"No More"

he said with a

His lips parted hers with a kiss that invaded not just her mouth but her soul with the depth of desire it sparked. It demanded a response, insisting she yield to her aching emotions. She was breathless when the pressure ceased and he released her.

His mouth moved in a smile and Dayna realized that he was as breathless as she was, but his voice was steady when he said, "When you're through playing games, let me know."

"I'm not playing a game."

"Yes, you are," Brand answered. "With yourself."

Then he turned away and began to climb the long hill toward the house.

JENNIFER MIKELS
lives in Arizona with her husband and two sons. The fanaticism over sports runs high among the men in the family and Jennifer caught their fever. *Whirlwind* is her second Silhouette Special Edition.

Dear Reader,

Silhouette Special Editions are an exciting new line of contemporary romances from Silhouette Books. Special Editions are written specifically for our readers who want a story with heightened romantic tension.

Special Editions have all the elements you've enjoyed in Silhouette Romances and *more*. These stories concentrate on romance in a longer, more realistic and sophisticated way, and they feature greater sensual detail.

I hope you enjoy this book and all the wonderful romances from Silhouette. We welcome any suggestions or comments and invite you to write to us at the address below.

Karen Solem
Editor-in-Chief
Silhouette Books
P.O. Box 769
New York, N. Y. 10019

JENNIFER MIKELS
Whirlwind

Silhouette Special Edition
Published by Silhouette Books New York
America's Publisher of Contemporary Romance

Other Silhouette Books by Jennifer Mikels

A Sporting Affair

 SILHOUETTE BOOKS, a Division of Simon & Schuster, Inc.
1230 Avenue of the Americas, New York, N.Y. 10020

ISBN: 0-671-53624-9

First Silhouette Books printing October, 1983

10 9 8 7 6 5 4 3 2 1

Map by Ray Lundgren

America's Publisher of Contemporary Romance

Printed in the U.S.A.

BC91

Whirlwind

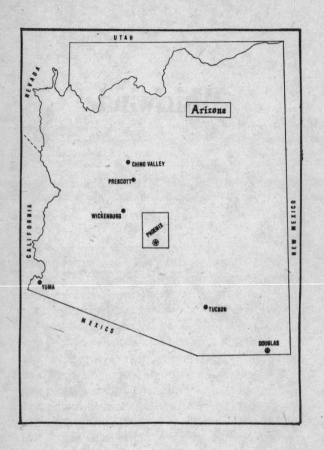

Chapter One

Brand Renfrow's cobalt-blue eyes narrowed as he contemplated what he had just seen and continued his caressing study of the woman's slender back and hips and the length of her shapely limbs.

The elevator doors opened and Brand stepped in, but as he turned, he decisively pushed the button that held the doors open. His eyes took in the woman's feather-cut tresses appreciatively. The burnt orange of the paisley-patterned dress she wore enhanced her coppery hair, bringing out striking red highlights. He couldn't bring himself to close the doors, for he had the vague feeling he had met her somewhere before, but then he rejected the thought—he wouldn't have forgotten this woman. The same thought had nagged him earlier that day when he had seen her for the first time by the hotel pool. A masculine quickening within his body made claim on his actions now. He was supposed to have met some friends five minutes ago in the lounge near the hotel's convention center, yet he stood spellbound.

That inner sense that told her she was being watched sent a sensation down Dayna's back. She turned away from the elderly gentleman she had met two days ago and raised her head, wondering how long the man in the elevator had been staring at her. The most disarming blue eyes she'd ever seen flickered appraisingly over her delicate patrician features, her bare shoulders, her low-cut dress. It wasn't a casual perusal. There wasn't a hint of politeness in his regard and a hidden spirit within her made her return his stare.

She regarded him with a boldness that matched his. He appeared to be in his thirties, though the faint lines at the corners of his eyes added character to his rugged magnetic good looks. The firm planes of his face were strongly chiseled and suntanned. Though dressed for a business meeting in a three-piece gray suit and powder-blue shirt, he had the demeanor of a sun worshipper, his tawny hair sun bleached to a silver color around his face. She sensed his virility, and his firm, authoritative stance conveyed that he was used to commanding respect and issuing orders. Yet his smile suggested a strong sense of humor. Dayna watched in fascination as his lips formed a half-smile, that lifted one corner of his mouth to reveal white, even teeth and a hint of dimples. It was a mischievously boyish smile but so sensuously devastating that she sensed she wasn't the only woman who'd ever felt her heart skip a beat from that grin. And the blue eyes sparkling at her with a devilish glint as the elevator doors closed certainly didn't help. With a puzzled frown over her own reaction, she turned her attention back to the stout, elderly man with the balding head.

Andrew Moran had an affable grin that broadened his round face. The smile became more pronounced now, indicating that he had noticed Dayna's visual exchange with the stranger. Moran and his wife, owners of a travel agency in Florida, had sat at Dayna's table for dinner the previous night. Together they had listened to the promotional speeches given by airlines representatives and various tour consultants about trips to the Caribbean, the Mediterranean, Alaska, Europe, and even one about a safari in Africa.

As co-owner with her father of the Palmer Travel Agency in Chicago, Dayna had been delegated long ago to do all the necessary traveling. In the last four months she had been away from Chicago more than ever before. Familiarization trips could hardly be considered relaxing, since she not only traveled the exact tour her clients would follow, but she also had to inspect the accommodations and dining establishments they would use on the way. This convention in Phoenix was the closest she'd come to a vacation in the last two years. She had enjoyed the camaraderie of others in the same profession who faced similar problems.

The Morans were two of those people. It was ironic. At twenty-seven, she was past the age of needing parental guidance, and her own father had stopped offering fatherly advice years ago. Yet the Morans seemed to look on anyone under thirty in a parental manner, and, good-naturedly, Dayna had accepted their constant stream of well-meaning words.

Not really wanting to hear a comment from Andrew Moran about the stranger, Dayna veiled the distinct tenseness she felt. Unconsciously, her hand tightened around the money Andrew had handed her before the stranger's presence distracted her as she stood outside the Morans' hotel room. She responded with a smile to his grateful words.

"Thank you, Dayna, for being our messenger girl."

"It's no problem," Dayna answered easily. She had agreed to bring the Morans milk later when she returned to her room.

"The hotel is so crowded tonight. I suppose the staff is probably just unable to get to all the requests for room service with a convention and a rodeo going on at the same time. I wouldn't bother you," he continued apologetically, "but we had an early dinner and unless Martha has her glass of milk before bed it takes her hours to get to sleep. With the plane flight back tomorrow, I thought she could use a good night's rest."

Dayna responded sympathetically. "I tried earlier to get room service. I couldn't get through, so I do understand. If I was settled for the night, I wouldn't go out again, either. I'll take care of it," she assured him in an accommodating tone acquired through years of making every effort to please clients. "I'll see you later."

She tucked the money into the side pocket of her shoulder bag and hurried down the hall toward her room to freshen up before meeting her companions for dinner.

As she reached the door, a masculine voice behind her caused her to jump. "Are you busy?"

Dayna whirled around, tensing for no real reason as she stared at the man who had been in the elevator just minutes ago. She realized she should have expected some form of pursuit—the set of his jaw was definitely that of an obstinate, determined man.

He flashed a smile, apparently quite aware of the disarming effect it had on the feminine sex. Dayna faced him with a quizzical expression. "We could," he said, reaching around her for the doorknob, "have room service bring up a bottle of champagne. Would that help you make a decision?"

Dayna's green eyes darkened. He was too fast even for her contemporary way of thinking, and she answered with a particular purpose in mind, "A bottle of Chateau Lafite Rothschild would be nice."

His fair brow arched in response to her request for a wine that far exceeded the ordinary man's pocketbook. "Is everything where you're concerned that expensive?"

"Okay, this has gone far enough," Dayna said, trying to keep her tone light, deciding it was the best action. "You're a little too fast," she said firmly. "I think the drink might be a bad idea. In fact, I think even talking to you might not be in my best interest."

He took a step closer, backing her against the door as he flashed a wicked grin. "What if I promised to make it worth your time and effort?"

"Wait a minute," she said with a nervous laugh. "First of all I don't know you. And second of all, I don't think we're on the same mental wavelength."

"You know as much about me as I know about you. For now, it's enough. I believe we were meant to meet," he said with a soft laugh. "You believe in destiny, don't you?"

"I believe we control our own destinies," Dayna answered firmly. "And you're not a part of mine."

He released an impatient sigh, a frown forming between his fair-colored brows. "What's the problem?"

Indignant, she fired a glare at him. "You seem to be the problem."

His eyes narrowed slightly and he leaned back against the wall beside the door to her room. He folded his arms across his chest in an arrogant stance, his blue eyes mocking her. "Come on, let's quit playing games. Doesn't your job at this convention include providing affectionate after-hours activity?"

"It does not!" Dayna retorted hotly. Her previous effort to be pleasant and remain polite waned. She felt slightly foolish standing in the hall having to explain herself to him, but now more than ever she sensed a commanding aura about him. He wasn't going to accept a simple no for an answer. "I'm a travel agent, here for the convention," she said emphatically. "And you have one of the most evil minds I've ever encountered. You're presumptuous and arrogant and . . ."

"Careful," he interjected. Hard chips of blue ice were staring at her, searching her face with a mixture of amusement and embarrassment, but there was no unsureness in his voice. "If we start name-calling, I'll win," he said with soft control. "For now, you do."

Dayna opened her mouth to hurl a retort, but it was never uttered. Instead, she stood fuming silently, glaring at his broad back as he walked away. Her head was throbbing, thinking of suitably derogatory adjectives for the most ill-mannered man she'd ever met. Whatever had given him the silly misconception that she was available for a price escaped her.

A frown remained on her face as she entered the room and tossed her shoulder bag on a nearby chair. Maybe she had indirectly caused the scene. Earlier today she had seen his smile for the first time. She had felt the same warm sensation coursing through her then, as she sat by poolside with her feet dangling in the water.

It had been the first time in the busy schedule of the convention she had had time just to sit and relax and work on acquiring a healthy suntan to take back home to a wintry Chicago.

Then those blue eyes had been hidden behind the green hue of sunglasses. She had felt them though, moving with the same denuding gaze, appraising every inch of soft flesh that her yellow bikini revealed.

Her womanly instincts had begun to stir and she had drunk in the virile bareness of his taut flesh, his body bronzed beneath the light-brown-colored mat of hair that covered his strong, sinewy chest. He had caught her staring, flashed that smile at her, and then with one agile motion dived into the water.

Good sense had dictated her immediate departure. But maybe her lazy stare had made the wrong impression. She gave her head a shake. She refused to accept any guilt because of a stranger's evil thoughts. It was a trap many women allowed themselves to fall into. They ended up feeling responsible, taking the blame for some man's advances when the fault clearly fell on his shoulders.

She had simply acted unwisely, staring at him too long. By nature she was cautious with men. Since she traveled so much, she had to be careful not to allow her attraction to the opposite sex to overpower her sound judgment. She'd held firmly to that principle, even during encounters with dashing Frenchmen or romantic Italians. It wasn't difficult. It seemed to her that most men were interested only in a cursory dalliance. They had one ultimate goal with a woman—getting her into the bedroom. Dayna knew that fly-by-night relationships wouldn't have time to develop into anything meaningful. If an attraction existed she knew it wasn't love. Love didn't come with such whirlwind velocity—at least not the lasting kind.

The phone rang, jarring her slightly. She took a few deep breaths to keep anger she felt toward the stranger out of her voice. Unexpectedly her hello was answered by her father's voice.

"Hi, yourself," she said, indicating her surprise. "How come you called? I'll be home tomorrow evening."

"How's the convention going?" Edward Palmer asked with a smile in his voice.

"A lot of the same cruises are being offered. The weather is beautiful, warm, and sunny. Karen and

Shelly are at a special seminar," she informed him in regard to the two associates from their agency who were also attending the convention. They were good friends of hers, her friendship with Karen going back to college days. "Mostly, I think they're being treated to the old routine that's been drummed into everyone for years: first and foremost, please the client."

Though he said it lightly, Dayna detected the serious concern that accompanied her father's next question. "You haven't met a Prince Charming by chance, have you?"

Dayna swallowed a sharp retort. It was an old argument between them. Her father was from the era of Gable and Lombard, Bogart and Bacall, Hepburn and Tracy—romantic couples who cherished the love of the other above all else. He really didn't understand today's society. A true romantic, he believed that romantic love actually existed. He just didn't understand why his beautiful twenty-seven-year-old daughter was still unattached. Dayna didn't really want to disillusion him but had hinted that finding a wife was the very last thing on the minds of today's men. Edward had tried to reason with Dayna about it. Personally he had liked some of the men she had dated, and though he guessed that a woman as beautiful as Dayna had probably fought off her share of Casanovas, he knew that if she continued to move at a snail's pace and insist on long courtships the right man might come along and then just give up in frustration.

Dayna had been adamant, though. Her parents' eighteen years together had instilled a strong feeling in her about marriage. She planned to marry

once, for always. The men she had met either
bored her after only months together or left her in
a state of disillusionment about love and romance,
coming on so fast with their maneuvers toward the
bedroom that her head practically whirled. She had
reached a point in her life where work had become
all-important. For her, men's promises of love
meant only one thing—sex. Though she knew the
depths of passion she could reach with the right
man, she didn't think a woman could know if he
was the right man after only a few weeks. Since
most men considered a learning period about a
woman a sacrifice of their time, Dayna had nearly
obliterated dating from her life. She knew that had
disturbed her father more than anything else. He
wanted her to be as happy as he had become in the
last few months. Dayna did her best to veil the
annoyance in her voice. "Father, is that what you
called about?"

He chuckled lightly. "No, of course not. I think
we have a problem, Dayna, that we've never
encountered before. I just received a call from
Harold Minter."

"Minter?" Dayna contemplated the name for
only a second. "Minter shiplines, exports, et
cetera?"

"That's the one," he answered. "It seems a few
problems cropped up during his wife's stay at the
dude ranch we recommended."

"I did the booking on that one," Dayna offered.
"She was there during the time you were in Dallas.
It's the Double R. We've booked reservations
there many times," Dayna said with a slight frown,
"and nothing ever happened before."

"I know we have," Edward agreed. "But this time we've got a problem. Minter's upset. It seems, Alexandria, his wife, complained about her treatment while she was there. Whether it's valid or just the anger of a woman scorned is something only she knows. She's claiming someone made improper advances."

One reddish-brown brow arched as Dayna had a dubious thought of her own, remembering a photograph she'd seen of Alexandria Minter on the society pages. "She's quite a bit younger than her husband, isn't she?"

"A good thirty years his junior. Since the Double R is in Arizona and you're there for the convention, I thought maybe you'd be willing to check on it. I don't think Melissa would appreciate another separation. And," he added, sensing what his daughter's next teasing remark would be, "I can't imagine Melissa Devereau spending a week with me in the desert riding horses while I tried to investigate."

Edward Palmer, though nearly sixty, was trim for his age. He had the flair and debonair demeanor of an international charmer. Since his wife's death nearly ten years ago, he had become quite a man-about-town, enjoying recently the appealing attributes of the owner of a world-famous cosmetics company, Melissa Devereau, who was only fifteen years older than his daughter. It seemed he was destined for marriage before Dayna.

Dayna couldn't help but laugh. Just the image of Melissa—always chic, always sophisticated, not a hair out of place—in such surroundings did seem ridiculous. She smiled as she agreed, "Melissa does look more the type to ride gondolas in Venice. But Dad, I just got back from a familiarization trip to Hawaii. I'm really not looking forward to living out of a suitcase again for a while."

"Couldn't you take it as a vacation?" he suggested. "You deserve one. And if something is being covered up, it shouldn't take more than two weeks to find out about it. All you have to do is relax and enjoy the Arizona sun. Get a nice suntan," he suggested. "I thought you'd have one when you came back from Hawaii. But bus tours don't exactly allow a great deal of time to bask in the sun. Anyway, find out if it's unwise for us to keep booking reservations at the Double R Guest Ranch. I really hope it's all a mistake. W.R. and I have known each other since before you were born. He's an old friend."

"Maybe Mrs. Minter made advances and the man wasn't cooperative enough to suit her?"

"There's always that possibility. And then again maybe not. It was the Double R foreman," Edward explained, "not some temporary cowhand."

"Is Minter really terribly upset?"

"For appearances' sake he's acting like an outraged husband, but I don't think he'll pursue the incident. I plan on doing so, however," he was quick to admit. "I find it hard to believe W.R. would allow any of his employees to overstep their position with one of the guests. However, because Alexandria Minter is married to a man who socializes with American notables and foreign nobility and we have in the past booked her on around-the-world cruises and never had any complaints, I think we're obligated to take this one seriously. As travel agents we're morally responsible to our clients."

"How do you know the owner?" Dayna questioned.

"I mentioned him before," Edward answered. "Reardon's wife was a childhood friend of your mother's. We met before you were born when he brought his family to Chicago for a trip. Because of our dealings with the Double R, I've kept up a long-distance friendship. He's a nice man, Dayna. And I suppose in a way that's part of the reason the Double R ended up being recommended by our agency originally. But it does have a high rating and we've received only good reports in the past."

Dayna sat back on the edge of the table next to the bed and asked an obvious question. "Since you know him personally, why don't you just call him about it?"

"A foreman has to have gained some of the owner's confidence or he wouldn't have that position. I don't want to call and ask questions without any proof. It would be insulting to Reardon."

In her silence, he sensed refusal and added as an incentive, "Snow flurries have started here again."

Dayna understood her father's dilemma. She laughed in response to his words and started unbuttoning her dress to change for dinner. "Is that supposed to be a persuasive weather report to get your own way?"

"Dayna," he appealed, "I am concerned about this. Do you realize how scandalous improper advances from some ranch hand could have been if this had turned into an adultery case and made the courts? Palmer Travel Agency would have been brought into it. I'll admit," he said quickly, "we wouldn't have been legally responsible, but some of our clients are in the same social circle as the Minters. I don't want them thinking we book reservations for wives or daughters at love communes."

Dayna laughed at his exaggeration. "I doubt they'd interpret it that way. If a grown woman decides to have an affair, that's her business. We're not camp counselors, Father."

"Dayna, listen to me."

She pressed fingertips against one temple and shook her head in a gesture of resignation. "All right, I'll go. What about reservations?"

"I'll take care of that. Since I know W.R. I should be able to pull a few strings and get you accommodations."

"It may be difficult," she reminded him. "I've always had to book reservations there at least a month in advance."

"Don't worry about it," he answered confidently. "I'm sure I can work something out. You're not still trying to get out of it, are you?"

"No," she said with a sigh. "If it will ease your mind, it's worth it."

"Is it really such a hardship?" he gibed teasingly.

"Well, to be honest, I think I would have chosen to vacation somewhere else."

"You could still take another vacation later in the year," he reminded her. "Do you want Karen to stay on so you'll have some company at the ranch? I'm not too sure, but I think it's fairly isolated."

Dayna smiled at his concession, aware that he was feeling guilty about insisting she go to the ranch. "Yes, I'd like that. Shelly too," Dayna added with a wicked smile.

She heard a hint of indulgence in his voice. He knew that she was deliberately leaving him short-handed at the agency. "Shelly too," he said good-naturedly, "my sweet witch."

Dayna laughed in response to the affectionate nickname he used only when exasperated with her. As she set the receiver down she stepped out of her dress. Why had she even fought him about it? she wondered wryly. After lolling in the balmy Hawaiian temperatures less than a week ago and watching the lazy surf roll in on Waikiki beach, she'd be foolish to hurry back to Chicago. Back home, she'd be shivering in freezing temperatures as she hurried across the Michigan Avenue Bridge. Instead she could enjoy the sunny, less bustling atmosphere of Phoenix and its surrounding countryside.

She walked to the hotel window. The view was a far cry from the familiar scene outside their travel agency window: the turn-of-the-century architecture of Chicago's old water tower and the spectacular mixture of white marble and steel and smoked-glass skyscrapers towering above with imposing authority.

There wasn't any hint of a bustling metropolis around her now. Phoenix was a sprawling city— only a few skyscrapers marked the central business center of the city, and the hotel she was staying in was outside the business district. Flanked by some of the city's finest private estates, the hotel offered

a view of Camelback Mountain, the adjacent golf
course, and a grass median lush with citrus trees
and flower gardens.

A glance at her wristwatch halted her day-
dreaming. Hurriedly, she changed from the cotton
sundress to a royal-blue voile. For a moment she
paused in the doorway, then fetched the name tag
she was supposed to be wearing throughout the
convention.

Dayna closed the door behind her, wondering if
she'd see a certain man again, then reproached
herself for even thinking about him.

Filled with thick-cushioned sofas and chairs, the
hotel lobby was lined with French doors that
offered a view and access to the patio of greenery
and flower gardens. Dayna headed for the restaurant adjacent to the convention-room wing. She
couldn't believe the number of passes she had
received from men since she'd arrived in Phoenix.
The convention she was attending had been sched-
uled at the same time as the annual Rodeo of
Rodeos, and the hotel lobby and the lounges had
become a Mecca for the hordes of swaggering
cowboys who were staying there. Though not
crude, they had been typically male. The hotel
wasn't for those on a modest income, and she
reasonably deduced these cowboys must have won
their share of rodeo purses to afford such comfortable accommodations.

She joined her friends at a table next to one of
the ceiling-to-floor windows with a view of the
immaculately landscaped lawns.

Dayna listened to their comments about the
seminar before telling them about her father's

phone call. Karen was pleased, but Shelly didn't respond, appearing preoccupied by the menu she was holding. An amiable young woman with soft brown, naturally curly hair, Shelly Berger had been working at the Palmer agency nearly four years. She greeted every situation with an easygoing cheerfulness, an attitude that even extended to her tendency toward plumpness. Though she would have liked to have a figure like Dayna's and the male attention it brought, she was already contemplating ordering a slice of cream pie for dessert. Feeling her companions' stares, she voiced her reluctance to Dayna's news. "I'm not too sure horses are my favorite companions."

With her long blond hair tied back and silver wire-rimmed glasses, Karen Hansen's appearance matched her serious, reserved manner. Married to an Air Force pilot who was currently stationed in American Samoa, she was taking advantage of every trip the agency offered until he returned and she could resume a normal married life. She had spent a year with an advertising agency before Dayna suggested that Karen should join her at the travel agency. Karen's quiet, calm manner had been ideal for handling the hectic crises that sometimes accompanied making last-minute accommodations. After five years with the travel agency, she was as enthusiastic as ever about her job and the benefits that went with it. She smiled in response to Shelly's comment, reminding her quickly, "You don't have to ride if you don't want to, Shelly. I think it's wonderful. I never expected the convention trip to be extended. Thanks, Dayna."

Dayna nodded, smiling, while the waitress delivered their salads. "It all might be conjecture, but my father was so upset. You know how he is. Obviously, unless I can assure him that nothing happened he'll continue to worry about the incident for the next couple of weeks the way he usually does. And I think you'll both agree there is something to be said for the milder March temperatures of Phoenix."

" 'Great' would suffice," Karen answered with a smile.

Some discussion followed about whether they'd packed sufficient clothing for an extended trip, but since all of them had overpacked in the first place, it was no problem. As they left the restaurant, they decided to meet in the lounge later. Karen and Shelly, in need of freshening their makeup, since they had gone to dinner right from the seminar, left Dayna at the elevator.

Dayna walked to the lounge next to the convention center, a room with a musical combo and a small center dance floor. When she entered, the piano player was offering his rendition of "Evergreen." Dayna sat down in one of the overstuffed chairs and took in the unusual high ceiling with its decagon shape. Wondering how long Karen and Shelly would take, she decided to order a Manhattan. She gestured for the waitress. No sooner had she received the woman's nod of acknowledgment when a soft male voice behind her asked, "Since you're alone, why don't you let me be the lucky candidate to buy you a drink?"

Dayna swiveled her chair away from the small table. She lifted her head and stared into the disturbing blue eyes of the stranger she had encountered earlier in the hall. She tensed inwardly but kept her voice steady, hoping she emanated cool poise. "I thought I made myself clear in the hallway."

"I guess I'm slow," he said with a smile. "Why don't we start over again, Dayna?"

Chapter Two

"How do you know my name?" She watched his gaze slide to her breasts. Though not low cut, the dress had a tantalizing V neckline. She looked down self-consciously. Her breasts swelled above the lacy cups of her bra, but she realized the view was much more revealing to her eyes than it could possibly be to anyone else's. She restrained the rush of color her own actions brought to her face as she met his eyes, now glinting with amusement.

"Your name tag. Dayna Palmer," he said, in a gently mocking voice. "Unfortunately, you weren't wearing it earlier this evening. I'm sorry if I came on too strong, if I offended you. Now, may I buy that drink?"

With the knowledge that Karen and Shelly would soon be joining her and there would be safety in numbers if he proved to be not contrite at all about his earlier manner, she nodded. The minute he sat down and unbuttoned his suit jacket, her eyes involuntarily were drawn to the lean waistline emphasized by the suit vest, and she questioned her own wisdom. She wasn't prone to such physical awareness of a man. For her own peace of mind, she said decisively, "One drink can't do any harm." She waited until he placed an order for her Manhattan and a beer for himself. "Since you know my name, don't you think I should know yours?"

"Brand Renfrow." Quickly, he corrected himself with a self-deprecating grin. "Actually, it's Brandon, but the nickname came early in life and never left."

Dayna nodded with understanding. "My father did the same to me. I've been trying to get away from the wicked nickname ever since. Tell me, are you in the city on business?"

He paused before answering, waiting until their drinks were set before them. Dayna ate the cherry in hers while he took a large swallow of his beer. "Yes, I am."

"Most of the guests seem to be here for the rodeo."

She saw, through lowered lids, his mouth quirking in an amused smile that indicated he understood what she was trying to convey. If he was interested in anything more than pleasant conversation, he might as well leave now and pursue some other woman in the room. "In a way, so am I."

Dayna arched a brow in surprise. "You don't look like a cowboy," she remarked, her glance taking in his expensive suit. "Tell me," she said half-sarcastically, unable to disguise her annoyance at the breed of men whose obvious passes she had been enduring for the past two days, "you're not a participant in the rodeo?"

He smiled and shook his head. "What kind of convention are you here for?" His brows knitted as he examined Dayna's name tag. He answered his own question. "A travel agents'." At her nod, he asked with a smile, "Have you seen any of the rodeo events?"

"No, but I've seen enough cowboys to last me a lifetime."

A silent laugh preceded his next comment. "I can imagine the panting looks you've received. An expensive, long-stemmed rose," he added as he looked down at her crossed legs. Dayna ignored his suggestive look and was relieved when he switched to a more neutral subject. "Where are you from?"

"Chicago."

"A big-city girl." He leaned back in his chair. "You're just used to a smoother line. All men give it a try. Some just believe pretty lines and subtle games are part of it. Wranglers are used to a simple, homespun look—wildflowers, daisies. And you're used to innuendos," he said with a knowing smile. "The approach may be slower where you're from, the tactics not so obvious, but they're all looking for the same thing."

"Since you're defending cowboys, I assume you know some."

"I'm not defending them. They're just not all bad."

Dayna shrugged a shoulder and changed the

subject back to him. "You said you were in town on business and it had to do with the rodeo."

His eyes locked with hers again, signaling that he wasn't quite willing to let go of the mood that had begun to build between them. That one look filled her with the desire to know the sinewy strength of his embrace and the taste of his lips before the evening ended. Dayna broke the visual exchange and looked down into her glass.

"I've seen a few of the events," he began to explain, "but what really drew me to Phoenix was the computer system they're using for it. I'm compiling information for a much smaller rodeo. They have quite a computer system here. Competitors—including those from out-of-state—can call in, indicate which events they want to enter, and the computer supplies them with schedules of the different competitions and the animal they'll be matched with on those specific dates. For some, the purse might not be big enough to warrant the travel time; others might have drawn a particular animal who they know won't be worth the time and effort."

Dayna shook her head in amazement. "It's unbelievable. We use computers all the time to secure accommodations, but who'd ever expect something as symbolically Old West and Country as rodeo competition to be right at home in the Computer Age."

Brand smiled back. "I suppose it does seem out of place. But time and experience improve methods."

Dayna smiled to herself. Talk about smooth. He had brought conversation to what he wanted without her even being aware of it. "How come you haven't slipped into the usual dialogue?" she asked. "Don't you know there's a set pattern to what a man says when he tries to pick up a woman in a bar?"

Amusement filled his voice. "Do you visit bars often?"

"No, but the dialogue usually includes, 'What's your sign?' "

A broad smile curved his masculine lips and his shoulders shook slightly with silent mirth. "Is that what you think I'm doing?"

"Aren't you?" Dayna asked with a challenging smile.

He cleared his throat and obligingly asked, "Okay, what's your sign?"

"Really, that's not necessary," Dayna said with a laugh.

"Come on, we'll play a little game. What's your horoscope sign?" Dayna shook her head, not believing they were going to have such silly conversation. But Brand persisted. "You look," he said, his eyes narrowing slightly in contemplation, "like a Taurus to me."

"That's right," Dayna answered, unable to veil her surprise. "How did you know that?"

"Taurus women are passionate ladies, sensuous looking and naturally friendly. You *definitely* look like a Taurus."

An impish sparkle danced in her eyes. "They're also very disciplined and reflective."

"I know," he answered with a wry grin. "It's a shame. They do tend to analyze everything, don't they?"

Her gaze met his, a touch of amusement in her voice as she answered, "Yes, they do." She took a sip of her drink. From behind lowered lids, she saw his speculative look shift to one of resignation. "So, what's your sign?" she asked, enjoying the light conversation now that she was sure she was in control.

"Leo," he answered with a grin that indicated he expected some taunting remark in return.

Not wanting to disappoint him, Dayna nodded her head. "Leo, the lion. I should have guessed. Leo people thrive on authority, are natural leaders, and they're also inclined to be arrogant with a strong sense of self-importance," she added with soft laughter.

An amused smile brightened his blue eyes. "Go on," he urged with a teasing lilt.

"That's all I know," Dayna said with a shrug. She wasn't an ardent follower of astrology, but one man she had dated was a Leo and he had been eager to tell her about himself. She remembered quite vividly some of his boastful comments. "They're supposed to be strong and handsome and definitely decision makers."

"Do you think those characteristics fit me?"

"I really don't think I know you well enough to answer that. But," she replied lightly, willing to flatter his ego somewhat, "I guess they do."

"You forgot to mention what's most important," he stated, restraining a smile. "They're tender and are known to have wild imaginations in *certain areas.*"

Dayna's green eyes danced with humor. "Certain areas?" she asked, holding back laughter.

"Definitely certain areas," Brand answered, deadpan, but then his lips widened into a smile. As a soft laugh slipped out, Dayna let her own mirth escape.

It had been a long time since she had felt so light in spirit, just sharing a silly conversation with a man. But then it had been a long time since she had shared her time with any man who didn't take his own ability to charm the socks off her seriously. Brand was laughing at himself, and she was enjoying their game of words. "I do know," she offered, to keep the game going, "that Leo people move along at a headstrong pace like a train that won't stop for anything."

"It sounds as if I'm not the first Leo you've ever met."

"You aren't," Dayna answered matter-of-factly.

"I have a feeling I should hope you really don't believe in horoscopes."

"Why do you say that?"

"Well, if *he* didn't leave you with fond memories, you might automatically dislike all men born under that sign."

"I don't believe in it," Dayna assured him.

"A more impulsive woman might. But you're not the kind of woman who acts without conscious thought, are you?"

"No, I'm not," Dayna answered. Good sense told her to leave now. The mood had changed between them, the lightness suddenly gone. Though she hadn't made any revealing move, Brand discerned by her silence that within minutes he might be sitting alone.

He leaned forward, rested his elbows on the

table, and reached for her hand. Dayna's head came up quickly, the touch of his hand on hers sending a shock through her. "I'm also a palm reader," Brand offered quickly.

Dayna rolled her eyes with disbelief, but her instincts were triggered by that first initial contact with his flesh and she stared down at her hand, unable to jerk it away from his warm one. He held onto it firmly and leaned further forward, forcing her to do the same. Their heads were bent, nearly touching, as Brand looked down at her palm in the flickering light of the candle on the table.

"Let's see," he said, holding her hand with one of his while the thumb of his other hand stroked one of the prominent lines on her palm, in a slow suggestive motion. While his attention was directed at her hand, she openly perused his face, taking in the soft lines that crinkled at the corners of his eyes from days of squinting against a bright sun, and the tan lightly textured skin. The tan color made the blue of his eyes appear even brighter.

Dayna's brief reverie was broken as she became aware that Brand was gazing intently at her. His eyes glinted, showing his appreciation of the sight before him.

"What do you see?" Dayna asked, drawing a deep breath only after his blond head bent again.

"By your heart line, I see there's been a string of broken hearts in your life."

Dayna chided him lightly. "That's not what you're supposed to find out from studying it."

"Including mine," he said softly, ignoring her amused reproof. His fair brows knitted with feigned seriousness over what he was doing. He

pointed to a spot on her palm. "See this here?" he
asked and Dayna instinctively hunched closer.
"There's a line right here that connects with your
life line. That's a mark of destiny." He smiled,
looking up at her, his breath warm on her face. "It
says on your palm that we were supposed to meet."
Strands of hair on her forehead fluttered as he
spoke, his lips so close they could have kissed.
Dayna deliberately kept her gaze fixed on her
palm, but she could feel his intense stare as his
thumb moved to another line. "This is your love
line."

Before she was aware he was doing it, he drew
her hand to his mouth and his lips caressed her
palm. The sensuousness of the gesture had an
almost mesmerizing effect on her. It was erotically
intimate, and Dayna quickly slid her hand away.

Self-conscious warmth heated her face. She
stared at the drink before her, aware of an almost
compelling attraction between them. She knew her
arousal was obvious, and she wished every light in
the room would suddenly dim.

"Don't be embarrassed," he said with a whisper.
"I feel it too. I've felt it since the first moment I saw
you."

Dayna took a long drink of her Manhattan. As
she set the glass down again, she faced him with a
pretense of steadiness that she didn't really feel. "I
don't know what you're talking about."

His rueful smile almost made her wish she could
take the words back. He looked over his shoulder
in the direction of the combo and the small dance
floor. "Would you like to dance?" he asked.

The music was soft and tempting, and she sensed

her softness might be too tempting to him if he were to hold her close, even under the pretense of dancing.

"I don't think so."

"I promise I won't step on your toes," he said lightly, tilting his head to see her face as she looked down.

She chided herself for the feeling of cowardice that surged through her as she tried to meet his gaze. "It's not that," she answered, looking toward the lounge entrance, and wondering what was detaining Karen and Shelly. "I'm supposed to meet friends."

"A male friend?"

"No." Dayna shook her head. "Associates who are also here for the convention."

"Good," he said in a relieved tone. "I wouldn't want to have to prove I'm gallant and brave by fighting him just for something as innocent as a dance." He shoved back his chair and rose to his feet as if she had already given her acceptance. "One dance," he said with a mocking smile as he moved behind her chair. "One dance, like one drink, can't do any harm." Dayna stifled a smile over his gibe regarding her reluctance earlier to let him buy her a drink. But as he pulled out her chair and she rose to her feet, standing only inches from him, she felt again the magnetic spell he was weaving around her. No amount of reason or good sense seemed capable of overcoming the attraction that existed between them.

She drew a deep breath as they reached the dance floor and she stepped into his arms. It was music for lovers, music meant to lull the senses and

create a mood of enchantment as it moved the
couples at a dreamy swaying pace. The minute
Brand's arm came around her back and the heat of
his body touched her, she realized how easily she
could be drawn under that spell.

He held her politely, but his arm around her
waist was like an iron band, the strength both
protecting and threatening. Because of her ambiva-
lence, she allowed him to draw her closer so that
his hand was at the slender line of her waist. Forced
to rest her face against his, she felt his thighs
brushing against her. For some reason it felt so
natural, so comfortable to be with him. She knew
the danger in that kind of thinking and reminded
herself quickly that he was a stranger, a man she
would never see again. She drew back, forcing him
to allow some space between them.

Looking out at the others on the dance floor, she
tried to occupy her mind with thoughts of anything
but him. Most of the couples were also tightly
embraced.

"It seems to be a night for lovers," Brand said
softly, claiming Dayna's attention insistently.

She offered a weak smile. "I think it's more like
a night for cowboys on the prowl."

"You really are down on them, aren't you?" he
asked with soft laughter.

Dayna made a face. "In the last few days, I've
met my share of men who act as if they're still on
some round-up—whooping and howling."

"More accurately," Brand said with a knowing
look, "chasing and cornering. You might have
missed the experience of a lifetime." He smiled,

giving her waist an affectionate squeeze. "They're supposed to be good lovers."

Dayna looked up at him skeptically. "Who told you that?"

"A cowboy," Brand answered lightly.

Her laughter slipped out easily. She was drawn closer again and her senses seemed wrapped up in an awareness of him: the width of his shoulders, the scent of his after-shave lotion, the texture of his smoothly shaven jaw. She was too comfortable with him for her own good. Laughter came easily, their conversation was unrestrained. Never before had any man turned her head so easily. She was too wise, too experienced not to know that if she wasn't careful she might regret this evening.

When they returned to the table, Dayna made a motion to leave, but Brand ordered another drink for her before she had a chance to refuse.

"One more drink," he requested with a smile that was meant to elicit an agreeable nod from any woman. Dayna mentally shook her head. She was beginning to feel like a puppet. She was suddenly incapable of saying the word "no." When the second Manhattan was set before her, she was determined it would be the last drink they shared.

"Now," Brand said, "we've shared two drinks and a delightful dance. Do I qualify as a close-enough acquaintance to know your mysterious moniker?"

"Have you been dying of curiosity about my *nickname* all this time?"

"Waiting with bated breath," he answered, a hint of a smile curving his masculine lips.

"It's my father's nickname for me," she answered self-consciously, "and he only uses it when I've thoroughly exasperated him." She made a face, trying to restrain a blush but she knew her cheeks were becoming pinker. "It's not even a logical one. I mean I really don't know why he gave it to me."

His brow arched as Brand smiled with amusement over her lengthy explanation. Feeling silly suddenly, Dayna blurted out, "It's sweet witch."

His blue eyes narrowed, and Dayna knew he was reflecting on what she had said. She felt as if he was examining her soul, as a perceptive light glimmered in his eyes. "Kind of a contradictory combination," he mused.

Sensing that Brand had already made his own deductions, Dayna admitted, "He says I am."

"You are," Brand agreed easily, making Dayna wonder how he had gained this instantaneous insight. "You're fascinating. Because you're a study in contrasts. Obviously, since you own your own business and travel a great deal, you're a very independent, sophisticated lady—" he paused, teasing glints darkening the blue of his eyes as if he knew in advance what the result of his next words would be—"who blushes easily." Dayna looked down, fighting the heat that threatened to spread to her face. "Your father might not be wrong. In fact, I know for sure he isn't." Dayna kept her gaze fixed on her drink and removed the cherry. As she slid it into her mouth, he said softly, "Only a sweet witch could do what you've accomplished in less than a few hours."

She looked up. His blue eyes were fixed on her

lips with a look of warm preoccupation. A silent, sensuous message was conveyed as his eyes held hers. But she didn't feel threatened by it. If anything, she was battling sensuous feelings of her own. An unrecognized force had kept her there despite the warning of her inner, reasonable self— it wasn't the most sensible thing to do. She should get up now and leave. Nothing could come of this encounter. Yet she stayed—held by the special magic in his eyes—eyes that caressed her face as if making a mental picture of her.

Brand's voice broke into her thoughts. "You've cast some kind of spell over me. I think I fell in love with you at eleven o'clock this morning by the pool."

Much too realistic to take his words seriously, Dayna fought the sensation his comments aroused. With soft laughter, she answered, "If you only *think* you did, we're both still sane."

"You don't believe in love at first sight?"

"No," Dayna said. "That only happens in the movies."

"You're obviously a lady who's too sensible for that sort of frivolous thinking."

"Much too sensible," she answered quickly.

He gave an off-hand shrug, letting her response slide. Dayna smiled to herself. Harmless flirting could be fun, and that's all it was between them. She believed with some satisfaction that he had finally abandoned his approach and his goal, and that, accepting defeat, he would probably leave soon to find more compliant company.

Brand leaned back in his chair and swiveled it to the side, seemingly content to stay there for hours.

Bending his leg, he rested a heel on his knee and began asking her questions about the convention. Dayna filled him in on what she had been doing for the past two days, but she was somewhat skeptical. He was showing a sincere curiosity about a topic that should have bored anyone but another travel agent.

"How long is this convention supposed to last?"

"I leave tomorrow evening. And yourself?" she asked.

"I'll be gone by nine tomorrow morning. We could make a full night of it and spend the rest of our time here together," he said, flashing a suggestive smile.

Dayna laughed. "You never give up."

"See how much you know about me already. I've got a stubborn streak. You could date some men for months before becoming aware they possessed that trait."

"I need my sleep," she answered in response to his suggestion.

"Airplane flights are very restful."

"I don't sleep well unless I'm in bed," Dayna replied, but her smile lingered.

"I'd let you sleep—a little while." His gaze was filled with the same smoldering warmth she heard in his voice.

"I doubt it," Dayna answered, playing his game of words. "I think you're too persistent."

He laughed shortly before asking with more seriousness, "Are you headed back to Chicago?"

"No, I'm not. Believe it or not I'm off to a dude ranch."

A flicker of amusement crossed his face. "You don't look the type."

"That's what I thought, too. But my father has different ideas. He has a friend who owns a ranch. Since our agency recommends it, he thought it might be a nice place for me to take my vacation."

Brand chuckled. "That really is a mixture of business and pleasure. What's the name of it?"

"The Double R. Have you heard of it?" Dayna asked, wondering if a stranger might give her an objective opinion about the ranch.

"I've heard of it. It's near Wickenburg. There are a lot of guest ranches out that way." Brand shifted the conversation to the workings of a travel agency. She answered everything he asked but couldn't help smiling when he commented, "See, I wasn't wrong earlier. You do get paid to attend parties, don't you?"

"I guess that's true," Dayna said, finding some humor in the situation now. "But not private parties," she added, feeling both chilled and warmed by his gaze. Like caressing hands, it moved over her face and shoulders. Her years of experience handling men from all parts of the world had deserted her with this man. She worked hard to ignore his meaningful gaze. "My job is to make certain all phases of a client's vacation are enjoyable."

A smile curled one corner of his mouth. "I think we're even. With some difficulty, I've managed to remove my foot from my mouth. I'd say, though, you did make my stay here enjoyable today."

"What does that mean?" Dayna asked warily.

"It's very flattering to have a beautiful woman stare at you. Like you were doing this morning by the pool." Laughter edged his voice as he teased her. "I'll satisfy your curiosity any time you say, if it extends to more than what you could see."

"You definitely have a one-track mind. And, really," she chided, "you're very blunt." She veiled the embarrassment she felt at having been caught staring at him by offering a logical reason. "I was merely admiring your suntan."

"Good old Texas sun," he drawled with a feigned southwestern twang. He hunched forward again, resting his arms on the table. Small and circular, it was like the others in the room and meant to enhance the intimate atmosphere. His movement brought his face very close to hers. "And let's be honest. You'd be more offended, wouldn't you, if I didn't try to make a pass at you?"

"Do you always say exactly what you're thinking?"

Amusement leaped into his eyes. "Often."

She glanced at her watch, beginning to worry about Karen and Shelly. One drink had turned into a few, and the brief time she thought she'd spend with Brand had exceeded an hour. "I think you'll have to excuse me," she said, rising to her feet before he could offer any resistance. He was standing before Dayna could move away.

She held onto a smile, a token of politeness, as his hand touched her arm. It placed no real restraint on her, but the strength it possessed could be felt in the firm grip. Her green eyes met his squarely, conveying that she wasn't a female easily prone to intimidation. If he became difficult and spoiled the pleasurable time they had spent together with some macho move, she didn't plan on being as good-natured as she seemed.

His hand immediately dropped away. "Do you have to go so soon?"

"Yes, I do," Dayna answered, starting toward the elevator. Not surprised that he walked with her, she added, "I really should have left sooner. Thank you for buying me the drinks."

"It was my pleasure." He smiled in response and pushed the elevator button. "Are you sure you want to say good night?" he tried again, facing her with a look of mocking displeasure.

Dayna laughed, and with more truth than she'd expected when he first sat down by her, she said, "Even though brief, it was nice meeting you. But . . ."

"Always a but," he said, flashing a smile. "You've got to stop analyzing everything and just act on impulse."

If he only knew, she thought wryly. She was far from immune to his charm, and her fragile resistance seemed ready to break. There was an air of anticipation about their meeting like some cloud hovering over them just waiting to burst. His eyes moved to her lips now. Dayna sensed the kiss even before he lowered his head and his mouth drifted down to hers, but she didn't resist. As his arm came around her back and he drew her slightly to him, she slid her hands to his shoulders and responded to the mouth moving over hers in a slow, testing manner. His lips caressed hers gently before the pressure deepened. It was a persuasive, stirring kiss, one that could arouse a woman without much effort. A heady lightness caused Dayna to lean against him when he raised his head in response to the opening of elevator doors.

"Come with me." It was a soft, appealing command, and the pressure of his strong hand around her arm was urgent and persuasive. Her resolve almost wavered under the power of his will, but then she caught herself.

She asked with a light laugh, surprised at her own easy manner, "What can really happen in one night?"

"It could bring an eternity of tenderness and understanding," Brand answered easily, the soft huskiness of his voice more of a lure than his words.

"Or just a moment to remember," Dayna replied. But she didn't feel as sure of herself as she sounded. To touch his sinewy flesh and taste its saltiness would be an experience to remember.

She looked down at his hand, at the color of his flesh, so much darker than her own. It was a broad hand, strong yet gentle. She felt oddly safe with him even though she hardly knew him, and sensed he'd be a considerate and tender lover.

She blinked, abruptly dismissed the state of complacency that overwhelmed her, stunned that such sensuous thoughts had filled her own mind.

His gaze was again perusing her, but this time it was slow and raking, meant to make her aware of his thoughts. As his eyes moved down and then back up her length, his features softened. Her breath quickened. She wasn't an adolescent who had never been the object of sensuous visual passes. Yet she would be lying to herself now if she pretended she didn't want to know the warmth of his embrace, the consuming power of his body.

Dayna moved quickly away, more concerned over her own response than anything else. As she stepped into the elevator and faced Brand, she met his blue eyes and saw his rueful smile. "There is something to be said for a brief encounter."

With the same sureness he had shown throughout the few short hours they had been together, he responded, "I believe in destiny, Dayna. We'll meet again."

Chapter Three

*E*ye-squinting sunshine glared down on Dayna, blasting heat against her skin as she waited with Shelly and Karen outside the hotel for transportation to the Double R Guest Ranch.

Slipping on her sunglasses, Dayna experienced a momentary illusion of coolness, which was dispelled as she felt the fabric of her yellow dress sticking to her back, and rivulets of perspiration tickling the flesh between her breasts. She noticed she wasn't alone in her discomfort. Beads of perspiration had formed above Shelly's upper lip, and she felt her smooth, sophisticated coiffure—the result of concentrated effort in front of her mirror that morning—succumb to the pounding heat as her hair reverted to its naturally tightly curled state.

Dayna's gaze searched the cars in the hotel's vast

parking lot. She had tried not to think further about Brand after she left him, but now, with nothing to do until the ranch's car arrived, she found herself thinking about the evening before. She wasn't so naive that she didn't recognize a persuasive line when she heard it. She honestly had expected him to try harder to coax her to his room and was surprised when he hadn't. Even though their meeting was brief, it had been quite an experience. After the clash between them in the hallway, she never imagined she'd end up spending part of the evening with him or that she would be so receptive to his kiss. But his apology had soothed away her irritation with the blinking of an eye. From that moment on, the initial attraction she had felt for him had taken over. Somehow she sensed that it was just as well their encounter had been so brief. Too much excitement stirred within when she was with him. There was definitely a chemistry between them and with a little more mixing together quite an explosive formula could have been concocted.

She looked up and saw the blue van bearing the printed words "Double R Guest Ranch" in gold letters on the side panel. The driver was concealed by the tinted glass and the decorative screen on the windows, so they couldn't see him until the door opened and he came around the front of the van.

Standing nearly six feet tall, he lumbered toward them with slow steps. A pronounced paunch hung over the carved leather belt of his low-riding jeans, and the sleeves of his plaid shirt were rolled up to his forearms, revealing strong arms that belied his excess poundage. He appeared to be in his late fifties. He doffed his brown, soft-textured Stetson to display thin gray hair and bright brown eyes that glistened with humor. Deep lines were etched in his leathery skin as he smiled a greeting. "Welcome, ladies. Name's Roscoe T. Bonner. Bonnie for short. Right sorry I'm so late."

Dayna was slow to respond, not having really expected a typical cowboy to meet them.

Tilting his head, Bonnie asked, "You are the ladies from the city I was supposed to meet, aren't you?"

Dayna nodded as she noted the bowed legs that supported the man's huge frame.

It was all the response Bonnie needed to continue loquaciously. "Well, here now," he said, reaching for their luggage, "let me take these and get you aboard and out of this sun so you can get to the Double R before sunset. Prettiest time of the day," he added, as he opened the back door of the van and placed the luggage inside.

Despite his down-home attire and demeanor, he gallantly assisted each of them into the van. Dayna waited until they had pulled out of the private drive into the city's rush-hour traffic before asking, "Is it far?"

"Nope. Used to take less time, but that was way before all the people swarmed in on us and the speed limit got lowered."

Dayna smiled to herself, liking the man's amiable manner. She was quite certain Roscoe T. Bonner would tell them all about overpopulation and a lot of other things that didn't coincide with his way of thinking. She suddenly became aware that his keen, twinkling brown eyes were staring at her in the rear-view mirror.

With a questioning look, Dayna said, "I'm sorry. Did you say something to me?"

"Was saying I sure hope you ladies like your stay. Hope you'll forgive an old codger like myself for staring," he said, including Shelly and Karen even though his eyes were fixed on Dayna and his words were obviously meant for her. "I think you ladies may outdo the beauty of our sunset. Sure are the prettiest ladies I've seen in a long time. That's the most beautiful color hair, ma'am, I've ever seen. Looks like gold threads have been woven into that hair of yours."

Dayna thanked him for his compliment and responded teasingly, "I bet you say that to all the women."

Bonnie snorted, his head moving back with mirth. "An old goat like me? No, ma'am," he said, his eyes twinkling with memories of past days. "I had my share of flings in my younger years. There's plenty of young bucks strutting around now who do that sort of thing." He winked at Dayna in the mirror. "I just flirt with the pretty girls now."

Dayna smiled with amusement, leaned her head back, and closed her eyes for a few minutes. She remained that way, not really listening to the conversation around her. Her mind's eye conjured up such a clear image of Brand that it was as if he stood before her, and she fought to dispel the image. From the things the others were saying, it seemed they were out in the country, and she opened her eyes. As far as the eye could see there was open land, sparsely covered by prickly totem pole cacti and desert bushes, straggly looking pale green foliage, and in the far distance, the hazy outline of jagged mountains.

"Can you accommodate many guests?" Shelly asked.

"We're kind of small compared to some of the resort ranches that have over a hundred guests. The whole spread's not small though," he said with a proud expression that revealed his years of loyalty. "It's one of the biggest in the state—still an honest-to-goodness cattle ranch. A new complex was built to accommodate guests, but there's still all the old buildings of the original ranch, and that's where the wranglers are most of the day. It's kind of like two worlds, and who you are pretty much determines which world you see. W.R.—Will Reardon, that is—gets so he knows every one of the guests by name. His thinking is that if everyone gets to know everyone else, they're more comfortable. We get a lot of regulars who return year after year because of that way of thinking. They get to feeling like it's home." He made a grimace. "And I don't think it's for Charlie Young's cooking. Not that it's bad, mind you. Sure wouldn't want you thinking you're going to starve. I guess it's good. Everyone says so. But me, I've always been partial to biscuits and gravy for breakfast, and dang nab it, only once in a while you'll find it on the menu, and that's only because our foreman has gone and ordered it."

Karen glanced at Dayna with a meaningful look. They weren't even at the ranch and already the foreman was being mentioned. Dayna's curiosity was piqued. "Is the foreman difficult to get along with?"

"Not really. Sometimes he's the most ornery foreman you'll ever meet if things aren't done right. But he's a man after my own heart who knows what should be served with his eggs."

Dayna grimaced over the idea of eggs and biscuits and gravy. Verbose as he was, Bonnie slid from one subject to the next. When his conversation turned to a description of some Indian ruins, Dayna directed her attention to the scenery again. Shelly's excited voice broke through her thoughts. "Is that it?"

"Sure is," Bonnie replied, conveying by his tone the pleasure he got when he looked at the ranch through the eyes of someone new.

Out in the middle of gently rolling hills and sparsely vegetated desert was a complex of buildings. A short drive over a curving, hilly dirt road soon again revealed the ranch. Sitting on a mesa were white adobe buildings with red Spanish tile rooftops. The multistory main lodge was flanked by motel-style accommodations and a few cottages. A circular flagstone path led the way to an immaculately kept golf course and a tennis court. In the distance was a stable and a small corral where some guests new to ranching were becoming acquainted with their new mode of transportation.

Dayna sat up in her seat, awed by the elegant resort atmosphere of the ranch. At the moment, she wasn't sure if she was disappointed that it wasn't more typically western or excited over the prospect of such a luxurious vacation. Glancing at Roscoe T. Bonner she found it hard to picture him in this environment. Dayna didn't need to ask Shelly her first impression of the resort. As Bonnie stopped the van, her eyes were fixed on an attractive man dressed in jeans but sporting an executive-styled haircut, indicating he was a city man and a guest.

Though it was cooler than in the city, the warmth of the setting sun lingered on the open desert. The heat of the day rose from the ground, penetrating the thin soles of Dayna's sandals.

An early evening breeze lifted a swirl of dust into the air. Standing beside the van, Dayna tucked her chin in to shield her face. The miniature whirlwind seemed to avoid her; nothing would spoil this friendly, welcoming scene.

When the minitornado had passed, Bonnie raised his head and watched the funnel of dirt journey over a hill. "Dust devils, they're called. Just come out of nowhere to swirl past you. Don't cause any real harm but sure are annoying for those who aren't used to them." He smiled, touching the brim of his Stetson. "We're just going to have to get you ladies some hats. Wear them low on your heads like this," he added, giving a brief demonstration, "and when one of those critters comes, you just bend your head down like so. Might as well get used to them. Dust devils are one of the natural charms of this part of the country," he said with a good-natured laugh.

Shelly and Karen nodded attentively, but Dayna was preoccupied with viewing the sights around her, noticing that there was no sign of a working ranch. Where was the other world that Bonnie had mentioned? Slowly she turned her head in response to Bonnie's voice as he suggested, "Why don't you ladies go stand on the covered porch? You'll be a lot cooler there while I get your suitcases."

Without hesitation they accepted his idea, and leading the way, Shelly tried to hurry around the front of the van, but the narrow heels of her shoes impeded her, slipping beneath her as she moved over the unsteady, shifting soil. She walked in this wobbling manner until she reached the flagstone walkway. Along with Karen, she moved onto the porch steps. Dayna was slower. As she approached the lodge, an old, dark-blue pickup raced around the corner of the building, shortcutting over unpaved ground and coming to a nerve-tingling, dust-blinding stop only inches away from her.

Particles of soft dust, the aftermath of the vehicle's abrupt stop, showered her. She choked on the finely powdered air, and, coughing ineffectually, waved it away from her face with her hand. A layer of grit clung to her skin as the sandy dirt settled to the ground again. The door of the pickup flew open and its driver jumped from the high seat of the cab.

Bonnie was also caught in the wake of the dusty cloud. He raised his bent head and, waving the dust away with his hat, he squinted in the driver's direction and grumbled, "We've got all kinds of dust devils."

Dayna's first sight of the speed demon from the pickup was a pair of well-broken-in and well-scuffed cowboy boots. The rest of his attire de-

clared he wasn't dressed just to offer the guests a
sight of a real western cowboy. He obviously did
his share of work around the cattle ranch.

Like Bonnie, he wore jeans, but his were dust-
shrouded and clung to his lean, masculine hips and
followed the hard contours of his long legs. A plain
leather belt with a large silver buckle held his blue
work shirt in place. Dusty and sweat-marked, the
open shirt neck revealed a chest covered by soft
brown hair. Because his worn and dusty hat was
pulled forward over his face, Dayna couldn't see
his grimace of distressed expression over the scene
he'd just caused.

He slammed the truck door and approached
them, an apology on the tip of his tongue. "Sorry
about that, but . . ." He cut his words short.

Dayna's breath caught in her throat as she lifted
her smarting eyes and met Brand's blue-eyed gaze.
Through the shock of momentary surprise she saw
his mocking amusement. "Still don't believe in
destiny, Dayna?"

Dayna held on tightly to her composure. He had
known she was coming to the ranch, and it now
seemed that he had intentionally kept silent about
certain facts just for his own private amusement.
Her eyes took in the jeans and work shirt once
more. Though he wasn't any less handsome now
than in the suit he had worn at the hotel, she fumed
inwardly, remembering he had also said nothing
during her remarks about cowboys. "Have you had
your fun?" she asked, unable to hide her irritation.

Seemingly unconcerned, he cocked the beige
western hat back on his head. The sun sprayed a

soft light on a portion of his hair, and once again a disturbing weakness swept through Dayna's entire body. She lowered her gaze, cognizant of just how much his good looks affected her, and brushed at the skirt of her dress. "You're really an imbecile," she added.

"I see we're back to name-calling. I said I was sorry," he repeated.

Shelly uttered a reply. "It's all right. We're okay."

Dayna had to swallow the words she really wanted to say but fired a question at him. "Do you work here?"

"It sounds as if you're about to pull rank on me," he speculated openly. "Yes, ma'am," he drawled with insolent mockery, laughter showing in his disturbing blue eyes. Her words about having her fill of cowboys came back to her. Had he been laughing at her throughout the whole conversation they'd shared? She could see nothing humorous in any part of the present situation, including the layer of grit clinging to her and the fact that her delicate sandals were covered with a quarter of an inch of sandy soil. Swiftly she averted her eyes and sought the only person she could appeal to.

"Mr. Bonner, is your employer nearby?"

Karen threw her a worried glance. Dayna knew she was questioning her agitated state over a simple mistake in timing.

Appearing baffled by her request, Bonnie sputtered, "Well—well, yes, ma'am, he is but . . ." Bonnie stopped himself, turning worried eyes on Brand. Brand responded as arrogantly as ever, it seemed to Dayna. Indifferently shrugging one shoulder and showing little concern, he left Bonnie in a quandary as to what to do.

Bonnie's indecision ended abruptly as the main lodge door opened and an older man appeared. "What's wrong here?"

Bonnie appeared relieved that someone else was there to referee and answered quickly. Offering the proper amount of respect to their guests, he said, "W.R., these ladies just arrived and—well— there's been a little, uh, trouble. A dust devil of our own welcomed them."

Tall, large-boned, with large facial features, William Reardon wasn't a handsome man. His most attractive physical characteristic was his thick mane of snow-white hair. He had a deep, authoritative voice, and Dayna was certain he would set an ill-mannered employee back a step or two. She knew her irritation stemmed from Brand's intentional silence in Phoenix, and the feeling urged her to get even somehow. "Sir," she began.

W.R. politely interrupted. "W.R., please."

Dayna gave him a wan smile, not wanting to direct her irritation with Brand at the pleasant and well-mannered man standing before her. "We'd just arrived, looking forward to an enjoyable and relaxing visit, when your employee came around the building as if he was on the last lap of the Indy 500."

A deep, rumbling chuckle was Brand's response although she hadn't meant to be funny. Dayna's green eyes flashed with annoyance, bringing Brand's laughter to an abrupt end but not removing the amused grin from his face.

Firmly, Dayna's eyes met his in a silent stand-off, but the blue eyes that narrowed at her in thoughtful contemplation were as disconcerting to her as his devilish smile. Trained to handle people and difficult situations, she was amazed that her poise was so shaky. She couldn't slow down the quickened pace of her heart which was only intensified by his sensuous gaze as it traveled down the length of her body. The warmth in his eyes was so intense it seemed to heat every inch of her flesh.

Unknowingly, W.R. came to her aid. "Ladies, I hope you'll forgive such an inhospitable welcome," he said, but his furrowed brow conveyed an inner confusion.

"Oh, that's all right," Shelly replied quickly.

Karen was also swift to answer. "Really," she assured W.R. with a smile, ignoring the gray layer of dust covering the tips of her shoes, "it was nothing."

Dayna could have wrung both their necks. A handsome man comes along and they turn to putty in his hands. Just like you, she reminded herself, remembering how responsive she had been with Brand.

Brand's mouth lifted in a winsome, gleaming smile meant to charm and placate. Turning to Shelly and Karen, he replied, "Thank you, ladies. That leaves only you, Dayna. What do you say? Am I forgiven?" he asked with a light mocking tone.

Dayna drew a deep breath, trying to counteract the warm glow of excitement sweeping through her. Grudgingly, she managed some pleasantry as she looked down at the front of her dress. "No harm done—I guess." Pointedly she added, "This time."

Brand's eyes danced with humor. "Thank you," he answered with exaggerated politeness, extending his hand in a gesture of peace. "I can see you've got the nature of a gracious lady."

Dayna stared at the large, sun-browned, calloused hand stretched toward her. The last thing she wanted to do was shake hands with him. Even that gesture seemed a mocking reminder that they were well past that stage. Her eyes flew to W.R. Was he deaf to the taunting sound in Brand's voice? If he was, Dayna couldn't tell. The Double R owner wore an ambiguous frown. With a resigned sigh, she knew she might as well shake Brand's hand and get the whole ridiculous situation over with. But when her palm was engulfed by the hugeness of his, she felt a sensual attraction even in this simple gesture.

Embarrassed by the intimacy conveyed through his caressing fingers, she tore her gaze away and jerked her hand free of him. Karen and Shelly stared at her with quizzical expressions, and Dayna knew that what had passed between her and Brand hadn't gone unnoticed.

To break the strained silence, she faced W.R. and quickly reinforced her poise with a slight lift of her chin. "I'm terribly sorry for making such a fuss over nothing."

W.R. flashed a broad smile at her. "I'm sorry it happened. May I welcome you ladies to the Double R and express my hope that the rest of your stay will be enjoyable." He sent an abbreviated glare at

Brand before returning his attention to Dayna. "And I hope nothing else will displease any of you while you stay with us. Let me show you inside and we'll see about your accommodations." He turned and opened the door behind him, tossing a quick command to Brand. "You'd better be off now and get those fences mended. Maybe out there you'll keep yourself out of trouble."

Hearing this censure, Dayna couldn't resist looking back over her shoulder and directing a satisfied smile at Brand. He responded to her smug expression and his employer's words with an indifferent, amused grin.

Dayna quickly climbed the rest of the steps. Bonnie followed, juggling their suitcases, but from the corner of her eye, Dayna saw W.R. frowning with perplexity. If an explanation became necessary, Dayna would offer it, but for now all she wanted was to escape Brand's unsettling presence.

The inside of the building was a complete contrast to its Spanish exterior. The massive, timbered lobby was totally western. Rich tones of natural woods, dark plank flooring, and old lanterns along with Indian handiwork and western artifacts added to the lobby's rustic atmosphere. Soft, cushioned sofas and chairs were grouped near an enormous stone fireplace and chimney, which rose twenty feet to a cathedral ceiling. This was the room's focal point and took up almost the entire length of one wall. Nearby, a heavy oak staircase led the way to the accommodations in the main lodge.

The loud sigh Bonnie emitted jarred Dayna. Having gathered their luggage, he had struggled up

the stairs and through the lodge door. Dayna
flashed an understanding smile at him. As he
maneuvered the luggage to the floor, he addressed
the woman behind the high-countered reception
desk. "Sara, these ladies just arrived."

The young woman behind the desk was dressed
in a powder-blue T-shirt and designer jeans and
had her long, dark hair tightly bound in a single
braid that reached the middle of her back. Even if
her hair hadn't been styled in that particular manner, the high cheekbones and strongly defined
features proudly declared her Indian ancestry.
"Names, please," she requested with a warm
smile.

Karen moved forward to supply the information.
As she did, W.R. approached them. "Ladies, let
me formally introduce myself. I'm really sorry for
such an oversight." Extending his hand to Dayna
first, he said, "William Reardon—W.R. to my
friends, and I hope that will include the three of
you."

Dayna accepted his hand. Wanting to offer a
better impression than she first had made, she
smiled brightly, but it faded quickly as she caught
sight of Brand standing near the doorway. "Dayna
Palmer, W.R.," she replied, using the informal
address offered and bringing a wide grin to W.R.'s
face. She liked him immediately and understood
now why her father showed such concern about the
ranch. "I understand you know my father, Edward
Palmer."

"You're Ed's daughter," he said with a wry
expression. "I should have realized. We've been

anticipating your arrival ever since your father called about accommodations." He winked conspiratorially at her. "All that proud father of yours talked about when we saw each other recently was his daughter and how competently she ran the travel agency."

"Thank you," Dayna answered with a smile, but her eyes were fixed on Brand.

Noticing that her attention had shifted, W.R. gestured slightly with his head back over his shoulder. "The wrangler behind me who made such a disruptive greeting is the man in charge of the spread, the foreman. You'll have to forgive him," he explained. "He tends to act like a charging bull at times."

He said more, but his words were lost to her. Brand was the foreman, the man the Minters had complained about. She stared thoughtfully at him and tried to remember if she had told him her reason for visiting the ranch when they were together in Phoenix. She hadn't, and now she was glad that she had shown some restraint. Having seen how fast he worked and how arrogant he could be, she found Mrs. Minter's complaint suddenly more believable.

Brand took a step forward, flashing a potently sexy smile at Dayna. "We've met. I didn't make a very good first impression on her," he said with a smile that indicated no ruefulness. "Though we did make some progress toward amiability, didn't we?"

Dayna held a tight rein on the warmth of embarrassment threatening to redden her face. "Amiability" seemed a mild description for the emotion she'd felt when he'd kissed her. Even so, she nodded in assent, but his smile was just too much. A knowing confidence emanated from him, conveying just what he meant by amiability. Her heart thundered in her chest as she realized just how much time he would have now to gently persuade her.

She turned away, trying to appear indifferent. Behind her she heard Brand tell W.R., "I'll meet you in the office."

Dayna couldn't resist looking over her shoulder. He moved away with easy strides across the wood floor covered by an enormous turquoise, gray, and white Indian rug.

Through the huge window that separated the office from the lobby, Dayna watched him settle into a chair in front of the desk and stretch out, crossing his legs at the ankles. She was railing at herself for following his movements when suddenly his blue eyes were turned to stare insolently back at her. She quickly looked away, pretending an interest in an enormous primitive-looking Indian weaving hanging on one of the walls. Somehow, despite her inner turmoil, she managed a smile in response to W.R.'s comment.

"I'll see you ladies at dinner. It's served at six-thirty. Now, if you'll excuse me, it seems I have some business to discuss."

For all her outward composure, Dayna sensed the last thing she would do on this particular vacation was relax. She kept her gaze averted from Brand, but all the while she felt that intense blue gaze resting on her speculatively.

With a mental growl, Dayna moved toward the lobby desk. From the moment he had met her, Brand had been very direct, his determined interest in her so obviously sensual that a person had to be blind not to see it.

She joined Karen and watched Bonnie's silent grumbling expression as he eyed their luggage. Despite her disturbing thoughts, Dayna had to smile at his pained look as he regarded the quantity of luggage he had to contend with.

The door of the lodge opened and a ranch hand entered. The man headed for a door marked "Employees Only," but Bonnie yelled out like a top sergeant, "Hank, get over here right now. It's about time you showed up."

"Huh?" the man answered in bewilderment but hurried over. "Nobody told me to come here. I was just going to see Charlie about supplies."

Dayna watched with amusement as Bonnie wangled the ranch hand into helping. "Oh, well, my mistake, Hank. You can see Charlie later, though. Come on and give me a hand with this luggage. You don't want these lovely ladies standing around here any longer and thinking bad of us, now do you?"

Dayna smiled as Hank tipped his hat and rushed to pick up the bags at Dayna's feet. "No way, Bonnie. All you had to do was say that some pretty lady needed her luggage carried and I would have come running."

Bonnie rolled his eyes upward at the ranch hand's flattering words. "I was sure you'd feel that way, Hank," he remarked, making a face.

Absently, Dayna listened to Shelly's excited chatter as they ascended the stairs. But as she paused on one step and glanced back, the cool air of the lodge seemed to grow warmer. A commanding blue gaze held her tensely still. Leaning against the doorjamb of W.R.'s office, Brand mouthed one word at her: "Destiny."

An odd clamminess dampened the back of her neck as she felt the same electrifying shock she'd experienced when he shook her hand.

She grabbed the banister to steady herself and whirled away from his devilish grin, wondering what had made her respond to the silent command of his eyes to turn around. There was no plausible explanation, but then she had reacted unpredictably ever since she'd met him.

As they walked through the long hall on the second floor, frequent interruptions in their progress soon dispelled her uncomfortable feelings. Bonnie's description of the guests was accurate. Everyone seemed eager to meet and become better acquainted with new guests. Bonnie was a congenial master of introductions, and he made them feel as though the various guests were members of his family.

It was going to be an unusual vacation for more reasons than one, Dayna thought. A heart-stirring event, at least as far as Shelly was concerned, occurred on the way to their room.

Bonnie again stopped their progress to introduce them to Martin Randolph, a young accountant from New York. Although their conversation with him was brief, Dayna learned that he was twenty-nine, single, as interested in astronomy as Shelly was, and, by the sparkle in his dark eyes behind aviator-styled glasses, more than casually interested in Shelly.

Dayna knew Shelly would have been happy to spend the next two weeks right where they were, standing in the hall talking to Martin, but she was relieved when Bonnie finally showed them into their room. He set the luggage down and then, with a tip of his hat, said he'd see them at dinner.

Excited conversation flowed as Shelly and Karen discussed the previous hour. While they talked, Dayna decided to unpack. She slipped out of her high heels and viewed the room. Set up in the manner of a suite, it was an extremely large, rectangular room painted a soft tan. It easily accommodated two double beds, a writing desk, a chest of drawers, and—on one side of the room—a settee and an overstuffed chair. Although three single women would be occupying it for the next two weeks, the fireplace and the large window with a spectacular view indicated it could have just as easily been a romantic haven for lovers. Earthy, wheat-colored carpeting, refurbished oak furniture of another century, and baskets of dried wildflowers decorated the room.

Dayna lifted her suitcase onto the bed while Karen took in the view from the window. "I couldn't believe the shape of Bonnie's legs when I first saw him," Karen commented.

"I know what you mean," Shelly replied and then added to show she wasn't making fun of him, "He's nice. In fact, everyone here is. W.R. seems to be the true cattle-baron type. And I thought Martin Randolph was very nice," she said in an overly reserved tone.

Karen lifted a brow at her. "Nice? Just nice, Shelly?"

"Oh, stop it." Shelly giggled, sitting on the edge of the bed next to Dayna's suitcase. "He did seem a little interested, didn't he?" she asked hopefully.

"Definitely a little interested," Karen assured her. She looked at Dayna who was removing a green dress from her suitcase and securing it on a hanger. "Someone else seemed a little interested in someone too."

Dayna looked up slowly, responding to the sudden silence that followed Karen's remark. "Are you talking about the foreman?"

Stretching the word out, Karen said with a smirk, "We-e-ll he could barely take his eyes off you."

"I don't believe this conversation. You expect me to be thrilled about a cowboy leering at me? Hardly," she said, answering her own question as she turned her attention back to unpacking. "He practically strips me naked when he looks at me."

Karen smiled slightly, one of her fair brows rising in response to Dayna's denials. "What really upsets you is the way you crumble under his gaze. The man's just got sensuous eyes. He's gorgeous and you know it."

Dayna remarked with a wry face, "I'm still not interested."

"I don't know why not. He's rugged and," Karen said, deepening her voice and making Shelly giggle, "sexy."

Remembering the deep-set blue eyes, bronze skin, and sun-streaked hair, Dayna had to agree mentally that Karen's description was accurate. "He might be all that. But I think it's important to remember he's also the foreman Alexandria Minter complained about. And, though I considered this a vacation, I *am* supposed to find out about that."

"He said you've met?" Karen queried.

Dayna heaved a sigh. "Yes, we've met. Brand is the man I told you about meeting in Phoenix."

Karen mouthed an "Oh."

Dayna sensed the uncomfortable remarks Karen might be tempted to make. When Dayna had finally found Karen and Shelly that evening in Phoenix, they had quickly apologized, telling Dayna they had been detained in the hall outside their room by a high-pressure representative of a tour company. The woman had insisted on showing them slides she had in her room and had used every effort to convince them how worthwhile it would be for Palmer Travel Agency to become affiliated with her company. Her tenacious sales tactics ended only when she realized the person she really needed to talk to, namely Dayna, wasn't there. Dayna's calm acceptance of being kept waiting had provoked questions from her friends, and she had told them about Brand, even about his suggestion that they spend the night together.

Seeing the curious look on Karen's face now, Dayna quickly grabbed her royal blue wrapper from the suitcase. "I'm going to take a shower and remove the dust that was stirred up by a certain thoughtless cowboy," she commented.

The shower had a refreshing, soothing effect as it

drove away Dayna's tenseness. She couldn't believe they had met again. Words Brand had said to
her came back. "I believe in destiny." "We'll meet
again." A cynical smile curved her mouth. He had
known darned well they would meet again.

The fragrance of perfumed soap floated into the
room as Dayna came out of the bathroom. She
moved to the mirror over the dresser and pulled
out the pins that held her hair back.

Lazily sprawled out on the bed and reading an
Arizona tourist guide book, Karen showed no
concern with hurrying to get ready for dinner. But
Shelly, in high spirits because of the attention she'd
received from Martin Randolph, whished by
Dayna. An excited glow warmed her complexion as
she nearly sang, "I'll take my shower now."

Dayna smiled as Shelly closed the bathroom
door behind her. Taking a seat on the edge of the
bed across from Karen, Dayna raked a hand
through her slightly damp hair. "Shelly's practically floating already. If Martin Randolph shows as
much interest at dinner toward her as he did
earlier, we may have to anchor her to the ground."

Karen laid the magazine aside. "Okay, now that
you're relaxed, what do you think about Alexandria Minter's story?"

Dayna made a face. "I have to take my father
seriously. But," she laughed lightly, "I figured it
was a good excuse to take a vacation."

Looking around her, Karen commented, "These
are beautiful accommodations." After a pause, she
said, "You seem to have an inside track on finding
out if Brand made 'uncalled-for advances' toward
the woman."

"Karen, don't say any more," Dayna appealed.

"You told me in Phoenix you enjoyed being with him; you wished there had been more time to really get to know him. It seems his thoughts about you are the same."

"Why don't we just forget I said that," Dayna answered much more sharply than she intended.

"Okay," Karen conceded lightly, but with a sigh of resignation. She moved to her suitcase. "I guess I'd better get showered and dressed, too." Looking over her shoulder at Dayna, she said teasingly, "I bet this is one time Shelly's going to go to dinner and not even care about the food."

Dayna's obstinate expression disappeared, and she chuckled. "I think you're right."

"I think I'm right about everything," Karen mumbled to herself, grabbing a light blue dress from her suitcase.

Chapter Four

It was an exceptionally warm night. Dayna stood before the mirror checking her appearance. Without any forethought she had chosen her green print spaghetti-strap sundress. Her bare shoulders shone with a soft tan, and her coppery hair glistened from her efforts with the brush. Using a light hand with her makeup, she applied a flattering shade of green eyeshadow, a coat of mascara, and the spice of a coral-colored lipstick. After applying one more coat of mascara, she eyed her reflection in the mirror critically.

The dress was much too alluring; it was seductive, gently following her slender curves, with a deep V-cut bodice that revealed a tantalizing hint of the swell of her breasts and exposed a great deal of soft skin. If Brand was at the barbecue tonight, the green dress would definitely entice his passionate nature. That was an understatement. Every time they had met, his eyes warmed like blue flames, his thoughts about her so intense only a blind person would have missed the silent message.

A wry expression settled on her face. She didn't really want his attention, did she? No, she didn't. Men like that used women. And Dayna had vowed a long time ago she wouldn't lose her self-respect because of some instant infatuation. Sensing her own susceptibility to his mischievous blue gaze and reckless smile, she was tempted to change her dress. She was still in a state of indecision when Karen and Shelly announced that they were ready. She dismissed her idea of changing, but as they went downstairs to the lobby, she hoped she wouldn't be sorry later.

Martin Randolph, looking very much at home in western slacks and a western-style plaid shirt, rose from the sofa in the lobby and rushed toward Shelly with a smile. "I waited for you. I hoped we could sit together at dinner."

Shelly's eyes grew wide as she gave an assenting nod. Hooking her arm through his, she flashed a beaming expression over her shoulder at Karen and Dayna.

Good-naturedly, Dayna exchanged a commiserating expression with Karen for their lack of male companionship, but then she saw someone else had been waiting just outside the high-ceilinged, timbered dining room and knew with a mixture of apprehension and excitement she wouldn't be lacking an escort for long.

"If I were you I would don your armor, Dayna," Karen mumbled out of the side of her mouth as she, too, saw Brand. "You're going to need some kind of protection against those blue eyes."

Dayna didn't have time to reply. Brand stepped forward, greeting Karen as she passed him, and then turned a smile on Dayna. She stopped before him. "I'm glad I ran into you," she said, drawing a pleased smile from him. "What I have to say won't take long."

"Sounds like I'm in for a tongue-lashing."

"You think all of this is very funny, don't you?" she asked, lifting her chin slightly. "I don't find it amusing when people deliberately try to make a fool out of me."

"Why don't you admit what's really upsetting you?" he said, taking a step closer so that the people who were passing them wouldn't hear. His blue eyes narrowed with speculation. "For a brief moment last night in Phoenix, you were contemplating going to bed with me—with a stranger. What really bothers you is that I know it. And you thought when you returned my kiss we'd never see each other again."

"You are really unbelievable," Dayna responded, unable to veil her own amazement over his blatant statement.

"Come on," he said with an easy smile, his hand lightly grabbing her elbow. "I'll walk you outside to the barbecue."

Dayna complied but said nothing as they walked through the dining room and out of the double glass doors to the flagstone walkway that led to the pool area.

Brand broke the silence between them with a comment as blunt as his others. "I could have gotten you into a compromising position with a little more persuasion."

"Oh, really?" Dayna replied, disbelieving humor edging her voice. "If that's so, why didn't you?" she challenged.

"Because once you mentioned that you were coming to this ranch, I knew I'd have a lot more time. So why rush it? This way we can move at your pace, and I'll know for sure you have no regrets."

"You are in for a rude awakening. Some women might find your direct tactics appealing, but I don't."

"I know," he answered with a smile. "You made that very clear in Phoenix when you were discussing cowboys and sidestepping me at the same time. That's why we'll move at your pace for a while. Patience is one of my best virtues."

"So is presumptuousness."

"How about if we pretend we've just met?" he asked lightly. "I find you fascinating, beautiful, and very desirable."

"And I find you extremely annoying," Dayna answered, forcing herself to meet his eyes.

"You didn't think that way about me last night when we were in Phoenix."

"I'm glad you brought that up. Just what were you doing there? Were you in Phoenix for that rodeo?"

"I was doing just what I told you," Brand said with a hint of annoyance. "I was there to get information from the central computer. We needed to know who would be participating in a rodeo the Double R hosts. And," he paused deliberately, drawing her close to him, "you know the answer to what I was doing there better than anyone else. I was the one making a fool out of myself with a certain beautiful redhead." His thoughtful expression placated her more than words ever could. "I *have* been coming on kind of strong, but you do have a devastating effect on a man."

His words triggered a response in her. Quickly, she reminded herself that soft lines couldn't be taken seriously. "Don't you think," she asked, "you could have told me you worked here?"

"It wasn't done maliciously, Dayna."

"I suppose neither was your offer to compensate me for my time?"

Brand sighed, a grimace flickering across his handsome face. Dayna watched with fascination as first a half-smile and then a disarming full grin curved his lips. She heard a strain of self-derision in his voice. "I was in the city for two nights and anticipating a little diversion and some compatible, receptive company for the evening."

"And you thought, on sight, that I would offer that? Do I really appear to be that kind of woman?"

A masculine chuckle answered her. "Not really." He shrugged one shoulder in response to Dayna's frown. "When I saw you, you were leaving a room and one fairly elderly gentleman was giving you a hug and handing you some money. I just jumped to the wrong conclusion."

"Oh, my God," Dayna groaned, understanding how her good deed had been misinterpreted. She couldn't restrain a faint smile as she explained, "He asked me to bring back coffee and a glass of milk. What you saw was a fatherly thank-you hug and the money to purchase what he and his wife wanted from the hotel coffee shop." With some satisfaction, Dayna took in Brand's expression of chagrin. "I told you I was a travel agent. Didn't you believe me?"

"Yes, I believed you," he answered with a hint of discomfort. "I just didn't know it then, remember?" His eyes slid to her breasts, and he smiled as he reached out and his fingertips lightly touched her bare flesh above the neckline of the dress. "You didn't have that name tag on."

Dayna looked away, drawing a deep breath, not believing how much just one quick touch from him could quicken her pulse. Her heart was racing furiously and she worked hard to keep her voice calm and not reveal the excitement coursing through her. "It is my job to be pleasant. Travel agents aren't supposed to be surly."

"Except with me," he said with an amused grin.

"You did provoke it."

"I tried to provoke a lot of other things, too," he said lightly. "Unfortunately I was unsuccessful." Dayna couldn't restrain a smile. He added, "Including a few smiles like that one. I really thought my past transgressions had been forgotten and we were on friendlier terms."

"We were," Dayna agreed. "But it's rather difficult to ignore blatant dishonesty."

An edge of irritation crept into his voice. "Okay," he sighed as if suddenly impatient, "before you get too carried away with this pious, 'I-can-do-no-wrong' attitude, let's talk really straight to one another." His eyes narrowed slightly, the hard glint in them recalling the authoritative, take-charge demeanor she'd first noticed. "Are you telling me you would have had a few drinks and danced with me if I had been honest about what I did for a living?" he asked with a skeptical look.

"I might have," Dayna replied defensively, lifting her chin slightly and meeting his eyes steadily.

"Aren't you being a little dishonest now? Remember, you're the one with all those very unfavorable views about cowboys," he reminded her mockingly.

"And you sat there in your three-piece suit nodding agreement with nearly everything I said," Dayna chided, unable to mask a smile as she saw the humor of it.

Brand chuckled softly in response. "I did, didn't I? Guess you were right about cowboys." His voice was tinged with humor as he shifted his hand on her waist. It was gentle but possessive, yet Dayna didn't fight it. Her brow knitted slightly when she realized she really didn't want to. Brand went on. "I tried to gain your interest in the oldest way a man knows how—catch your eye, smile at you, spend a little time talking and getting to know you." Dayna gave him a skeptical look. He'd wanted more and they both knew it. "Was what I did really so different from what you're used to?" he asked softly. "If anything, maybe I am too direct, maybe I rush a woman. But that's not really so objectionable, is it?" he asked, his gaze warmly touching every inch of her face. "I also told you something else. Do you remember what it was?"

Her heart skipped a beat. She remembered everything he had said and had to force herself not to look away from him. "Yes, I remember. You said that cowboys are supposed to be good lovers. Now that I know you're one, it sounds like you were doing some bragging." She made a face to take away the sting of her words and tried not to be caught by the soft lure of his voice. Her surroundings, the gentle breeze and the full moon in a star-filled sky were definitely capable of casting a romantic spell over even the most sensible person.

With a soft laugh, Brand answered, "You'll find out soon enough."

Her green eyes filled with amazement. "You don't really believe you and I . . . ?"

He flashed a smile. "A few more days together in Phoenix and we wouldn't even be having this discussion. It would be a fact."

For all the weakness flooding her, a strong-willed spirit balked at his comment. "I don't make a habit of going to bed with men I hardly know just for sexual satisfaction."

He took one step closer, his chest brushing against her breasts. "You don't think I'd offer romance?" he asked, the arm around her waist drawing her closer so that his thighs pressed against hers.

His hand rested on the curve of her hip. Dayna battled the strong sensations his nearness aroused. "That's not really reassuring. Whirlwind romances usually have devastating results."

With a mixture of disbelief and amusement, he asked, "Don't you ever read love stories? People meet sometimes by chance, fate steps in . . ."

"And they live happily ever after," Dayna interjected. His breath was warm against her face. "I know, love at first sight," she added in a bantering tone. She was trying to battle her own temptation to move closer to him and initiate a kiss.

"You don't believe in destiny or love at first sight?"

"No."

"You will," Brand said with confidence.

Dayna couldn't help but smile. "You're an incurable romantic."

"No, I'm a man who believes you take advantage of every opportunity that comes your way."

"And does that include taking advantage of every woman?"

One corner of his mouth quirked upward in response to her question. "Is that what you think I want to do with you?"

A long moment passed while his eyes never left her face. Dayna's stomach flipped over with uneasiness as his hand moved, his fingers gently touching the ends of her hair near her jaw. They slid upward slowly, touching her face with their warmth as they caressed the soft texture of her cheek. There was magic in the moment. It was as if they were alone in the world, the sounds of the party suddenly gone, the insects and soft breeze silent in anticipation. She was breathing heavily as she watched his head slowly descend toward her. The heat of his lips caressed her mouth and brushed first one corner and then the other. But as he moved to deepen the pressure, Dayna snapped herself out of the spell. She turned her face away and his lips touched her cheek instead.

"All right. For now we do it your way," he said with a grin, his dimples strongly defined at the corners of his mouth. "But I'm going to kiss you again. You know that. And turning your head away isn't going to stop me."

Dayna opened her mouth to offer some retort but his hand moved to the small of her back and urged her to walk. "It's almost time to eat," he commented with a casualness that made her wonder if she had imagined the special moment that had just passed.

He guided her to the area behind the lodge where the dark water of the pool glimmered under the moonlight but left her immediately when they reached W.R. She had expected it. In fact, she noted that his hand had left her back before they were in the company of others. She wondered whom these tokens of propriety were meant to impress.

She wasn't gullible; she'd certainly learned in just a few brief encounters that Brand moved at a fast pace, just like a lot of other men she had met. They were the type who made a practice of quick conquests.

And yet, aware as she was of this possibility, she wasn't showing a great deal of caution where Brand was concerned. If Mrs. Minter had told the truth, he was even more of an expert than the others Dayna had met. She was determined not to let the situation get out of hand. The most important thing for her to remember at the moment was that the strong reaction she felt toward him was more girlish infatuation than sensible mature emotions.

Calming her bewilderment, she wandered around the area. W.R. introduced her to a mixture of guests: honeymooners, a family of five, with two dreamy-eyed teenage girls whose eyes were fixed on the ranch hands seated around one of the picnic tables, retired couples who were regular yearly visitors, airline stewardesses from Albuquerque, and three college students who were avidly flirting with every single woman in sight.

A casual, festive mood permeated the atmosphere; the aroma of smoke from the mesquite-wood fire and the spicy tang of the barbecue sauce being used to baste a hindquarter of beef added to the party mood of southwestern hospitality. The melodic sounds of strumming guitars filled the night air in the huge yard. The colored lights of lanterns and fiery torches provided illumination.

Trapped in conversation with a schoolteacher from Ohio, a Mrs. Whitaker, an avid bird watcher, Dayna listened with half an ear and maintained a smile as the woman proceeded to describe every bird she'd ever seen, then burst into a vivid performance of bird calls that drew some attention to them. Dayna listened politely but managed without being observed to keep looking at Brand as he stood on the other side of the pool and mingled with other guests, smiling and talking to them with an ease that came from years of meeting and entertaining new acquaintances.

She scrutinized the perfect fit and expensive stitching of the dark blue shirt and beige brushed cotton jeans he was wearing. Dayna had to admit he had the kind of looks that could make the heart of any female throb. Some comments by the flight attendants during dinner confirmed Dayna's opinion. One of them in particular, Christy, a leggy brunette, declared her intention to "get to know Brand better."

Bonnie hadn't exaggerated when he spoke of the familylike atmosphere. Most of the men present were long-term employees of W.R. The show of comradeship and good-natured bantering that went on when they were introduced provided the guests with dinnertime humor. Although there was a cookhouse somewhere on the ranch, most of the ranch hands, those willing to spruce up, joined the guests for the dinner hour.

W.R. proved to be an interesting dinner companion, enlivening lulls in conversation with anecdotes about ranching and a few corny cowboy jokes. But Dayna was having a difficult time concentrating on what anyone was saying as she watched Christy leave their table and sidle up to Brand. Practically throwing herself at him, she didn't seem to give a thought to the conversation she had interrupted. No one really seemed to mind. The ranch hands received her with pleasant smiles, and it wasn't hard to understand why. She was wearing an extremely revealing hot-pink tube-top terry-cloth dress, which showed more of her curves than it covered. She sat on the edge of the table and faced Brand. Her tongue periodically moistened her lips as she talked to him and ran a caressing hand down his arm. Dayna rolled her eyes upward at the scene. The woman, batting her long, dark lashes, was using the tricks seen in a 1940s movie, and, like a fool, Brand seemed to be falling for them. He responded with an amused smile, but for a fleeting second, his gaze shifted, his eyes locking with Dayna's. She saw a flicker of sarcastic amusement in his perceptive eyes. He wasn't any more taken in by Christy's act than he was unaware that Dayna was watching him.

She looked quickly away, irritated with herself for being caught staring at him.

As if aware of Dayna's mood, Karen asked softly, "Is something wrong?"

Unable to explain what she couldn't even understand, Dayna forced a smile. "No. I see Shelly's with her accountant."

Karen glanced across the table at their friend, who was looking enchanted with Martin Randolph. "That's terrific, isn't it?" Karen sighed. "Leaves you and me." Her eyes shifted to Brand. "But I don't think we'll be a twosome for long, judging by the stare you're receiving from your cowboy."

"Will you stop that!" Dayna reproved in a low whisper, hoping no one at their table had heard Karen. "He's not *my* cowboy. Anyway," she said with a shrug of indifference, "he seems already to have fallen into another trap." Dayna gave Karen a side glance. "A cat's trap, I think."

"Meow! Dayna," Karen responded. "I've never heard you talk like that before. You almost sound jealous."

Dayna threw her a look of denial. Not interested in sharing more conversation with Brand, she turned to W.R. "Even though you're a friend of my father's, I really don't know much about you. Do you have a family?"

W.R. smiled. "A daughter who's married and has three children, and a son in Phoenix who's a lawyer. Tom never was very fond of the smells of ranching—like horse manure," he said with twinkling eyes. "He made it very clear early in life he would do anything associated with the ranch but the actual ranching. So he went to law school. He handles the legal matters for the ranch. It's worked out well. I'm sure of never getting cheated this way. My . . ." W.R. cut his words short as Bonnie passed by the table. He halted Bonnie with a question. "I didn't get a chance to ask Brand. I heard there was a ruckus right before dinner. Do you know what it was about?"

Bonnie laughed shortly. "I'm not sure what ruckus you're talking about." W.R. looked up at him with a questioning frown and Bonnie added lightly, "A Brahma busted out and jumped a six-foot fence. Brand was muttering and cussing all over the place while everyone else was running for cover, but the bull wasn't free for long. He outmaneuvered himself and got trapped in a bank near the river."

"Is the bull fenced in now?"

"Oh, yeah, but Brand swore he'd turn that bull into tomorrow night's supper if he had to chase it again."

Dayna smiled to herself, enjoying the trouble Brand had had until Karen reminded her of the danger of the situation when she commented, "They're big, aren't they—Brahma bulls?"

W.R. nodded. "Yes—it could have meant a trip to the hospital for someone." He looked at Bonnie. "Probably our matador foreman. Some bulls weigh close to two thousand pounds."

Bonnie grunted, appearing to take the incident very lightly. "That one sure was throwing and slamming his weight all over the place. There's a fence that's got to be repaired, and it rammed a water trough when one of the men dived for it."

"I'm almost afraid to ask," W.R. said. "What else happened?"

Bonnie commented matter-of-factly, "Brand had trouble with one of the ranch hands."

One of W.R.'s heavy white brows rose slightly, but he merely stated, "I'll ask him about it."

As Bonnie returned to the table where the other wranglers sat, Karen commented, "He's nice. Has he been with you long?"

"Nearly twenty years," W.R. smiled. "My children were just little tykes when he came. After my wife's death, he sort of became nursemaid, uncle, and friend."

Instinctively Dayna looked in Bonnie's direction, but it wasn't Bonnie she saw. Brand's disturbing penetrating blue eyes met hers. If she had thought the meal would prove less eventful than her arrival, she knew when she saw Brand rise and shove back his chair that she was wrong.

There was no mistaking where he was heading. Caught in the middle of a conversation, Dayna looked down at the forkful of Dutch apple pie in her hand and pretended she wasn't aware of his approach as she listened to W.R.

"I have to assume the reason for this vacation was the need for a quiet time, since you've probably already enjoyed most of the fun in the sun places like the Riviera or the Caribbean. Not that I'm complaining. I for one am very pleased to have such beauty gracing my ranch, but I'm surprised you chose a place lacking any nightlife."

Glancing at Shelly before she answered, Karen said with a sly smile, "We were glad for the chance to have a quiet vacation with country air and horseback riding."

"Oh, yes," Shelly agreed with feigned gaiety, "definitely horseback riding."

Karen snickered softly over her remark, but Martin took her words seriously. "I'm glad. I like to ride too. We'll have to do it tomorrow. Would you like that?"

Shelly's face came alive with enthusiasm and she beamed, "Yes, of course."

"And tennis," Martin added, putting his hand over hers on the table. "Do you play tennis?"

"Yes, but not well."

"Yes, you do," Dayna offered. "I'm really looking forward to some night playing. You have floodlit courts, don't you, W.R.?" He nodded, but she knew by the curious frown that settled on his face that he was going to ask more questions. She really didn't want to lie. Since W.R. was a close acquaintance of her father's, she had already been tempted a few times to tell him specifically why she was there. The thought passed quickly, for she was sure W.R., in fairness to his foreman, would tell Brand and there might be an attempt to cover up the truth. "My father actually was the one who suggested I take a vacation here," she offered with a smile, pleased she wasn't forced to lie.

Brand appeared, smiling a greeting to the receptive faces, but when he got to Dayna, his expression altered completely. Admiration glinted in his blue eyes as an uncomfortable silence descended on them. He was already pulling out the empty chair next to W.R. when he asked, "May I join you?"

As W.R. gave a consenting nod, Dayna looked down at the pie on her plate, doubting that she would finish it now. She noted W.R.'s rapid scrutiny, his gaze moving from her to Brand and back to her again.

Brand didn't notice. Leaning back in his chair in a relaxed pose, he looked at her in a way that sent a shiver up her spine. Dayna shifted slightly and poked with her fork at the pie on her plate. She knew the hot color of a girlish blush was sweeping over her face. Get hold of yourself, she mentally insisted. Her long, dark lashes lifted, and her green eyes shone with the determination to meet squarely the blue gaze so intent on her.

Dayna felt relieved as W.R. demanded everyone's attention and proceeded to make an announcement. "There'll be a rodeo in a few days, folks, mostly local cowhands competing, but it's sort of an annual event for the Double R. Hope all of you will come! And then in the evening, there'll be a western-style dinner, so make sure you're good and hungry."

Politely, Dayna waited until he was done and then pushed back her chair. She rose to her feet, and excused herself, pointedly avoiding a certain man's blue gaze. He had earlier put on a good act, but his attention to Christy dispelled any notions Dayna might have had that he wasn't just trying for the most available female. Slowly she worked her way away from the barbecue, exchanging pleasantries with some of the guests as she went. In her mind she had already classified Brand. He was the kind of man who would never be satisfied with only one woman's attention. She had met enough of that kind already.

She knew even before she saw him that Brand was behind her. She sensed his nearness a moment before she felt the warmth of his hand as it tightened around her waist. She wasn't really surprised by his pursuit. A man like him possessed an ego that wouldn't allow even one woman to escape. She whirled around, and his grip suddenly loosened as he saw the flash of indignation in her eyes.

She challenged him with that look, daring him to step out of line, and he couldn't restrain a smile or the mockery that gleamed in his eyes. "Would you like to go for a walk?" he asked innocently.

His amusement did more than nettle her. It set her pulse racing. As coolly and indifferently as she could, she answered, "No, I wouldn't. And if you'll excuse me, at the moment I have a greater need for . . ."

"For what? Anything but my company?" Brand finished. "You don't trust me, do you? You don't have a very forgiving nature, it seems," he mocked.

There was just too much attraction between them for her own good. Dayna replied defensively, in self-protection, "It's not very safe to be with you. I know how you jump to conclusions and make hasty decisions."

His eyes shone with amusement. On his face appeared a slow, taunting grin. "You're not proving very true to form. We've already discussed your very analytical nature, so what's your reason for this obvious anger at me? All I'm offering is friendship."

Dayna was tempted to scoff at him. She suppressed it, because she had to admit he sounded very honest. For a moment she wondered if she was misjudging him. There was an open quality about him that didn't jibe with the kind of man who, on a whim, tried to take advantage of a woman just to bolster his macho ego. Yet wasn't that what he had been doing with her ever since they met?

"With all your talk about destiny and other things," Dayna came back bluntly, "the word 'friendship' sounds preposterous. Why don't you just direct all this friendly energy toward someone who would appreciate it." Her gaze turned to Christy meaningfully.

"You don't want me to do that," Brand answered with a smile. "As a ranch employee I have some responsibility to help our guests if they need it. So all I'm really doing is my job. I'm here not only to make their stay pleasant but to answer their complaints."

"I could say you're the only one I need to complain about," she countered lightly.

He almost smiled; Dayna knew he was restraining it. Laughter sprang into his blue eyes as they sparkled with amusement over her remark. "And here I thought I was behaving myself."

"You jest," Dayna teased.

"What have I done?" he challenged.

"Nothing," Dayna answered. "Absolutely nothing."

"Is that the problem? If it is, you know it would

be my pleasure to find a remedy for the situation."
They reached the porch and he set a foot on the
first step. It kept Dayna from leaving him and
brought his face closer to hers.

Dayna knew his actions were deliberate. He was
trying to force a reaction from her and she struggled with herself, knowing it would be a mistake to
take notice of his move or to try to move around
him.

His blue eyes narrowed slightly. She had the
satisfaction of seeing a flicker of confusion in his
gaze and she smiled slightly, suddenly feeling in
control, but her triumph was short-lived.

Though only a second passed, it seemed an
eternity while his eyes slid over her bare shoulders
and settled on the plunging neckline of her dress.
"That's some dress you're wearing."

"I suppose out of politeness I should say thank
you for being leered at."

"I wasn't leering," he said with soft laughter. "I
was just being honest."

"If we're going to be really honest, I'm surprised
you noticed anything that wasn't in a shade of hot
pink. You know, it's easy to see why there's no
Mrs. Renfrow. You're really impossible."

"Are you asking me," Brand teased, "if there
is?"

"I'm not interested," she answered firmly. "But
did it ever occur to you that you might be infringing
on another man's territory? You never even bothered to find out if I was married."

His gaze went to her ring finger. "It's obvious
you aren't. Anyway, now would be a heck of a time
to start asking questions about your marital status.

That would be like closing the barn door after the horse was out. If there was a lover back in Chicago, you wouldn't have accepted my offer to buy you a drink."

"I assure you I don't lack for dates."

His eyes swept over her curves. "I never doubted for a minute that your social calendar wasn't booked solid. But I said 'lover,'" he reminded her mockingly. "There isn't one, is there?"

"Really, it's none of your business. I'm not asking you about your sex life."

He shrugged. "If you're interested, I'll answer your questions. I've known many women, but then I'm not sixteen years old, so that really isn't such a revealing statement from a man."

"I'm not concerned with the quantity of lovers you've had."

"Good," he answered lightly, "because I'm not concerned with your past loves, or how many men have stirred passion in you." His eyes deepened in color, the warmth and sensuousness of his thoughts spanning the distance between them. "All I care about is that I do," he said softly.

A tremor of expectation moved through her and Dayna suppressed it, revealing an unexpected trace of cynicism. "Aren't you going to offer false promises of love?"

Brand was quiet, his gaze searching her face. "You won't believe them," he answered softly.

"That's right, I wouldn't. I'm not naive, Brand, or easily swayed by a smooth line."

"I know," he replied, his tone unexpectedly serious. A moment of strained silence passed before he asked with a frown, "Why have you stereotyped me?"

"I haven't," Dayna responded quickly, her heart lurching because of his bluntness. She had stereotyped him and he knew it; she had marked him on sight as a womanizer.

"Whatever your thoughts are," Brand said, candid as ever, "I'll wager they're uncomplimentary." He gazed at her, pondering and searching for answers. "You're afraid to be with me," he noted with a touch of surprise.

"No, you're wrong," Dayna countered softly. "It's just that I don't believe you ever take no for an answer."

"I don't when I think the woman really wants to say yes."

"You think you have all the answers, don't you?"

"I do," Brand answered as if it were a fact. "You're just not receptive to them—yet." His eyes narrowed in contemplation. "Do you list all a man's monetary and personal assets on one side and all his human flaws on the other?"

The taunting tone of his voice was irritating. "It certainly would be wiser for a woman to do that than act like an insipid fool by plunging into relationships and letting her emotions control her life," she answered.

"Do you really believe you can choose the person you fall in love with?"

"I told you I control my own destiny."

She expected some smart retort, but Brand seemed to accept her statement with a nod of his head. "Yes, you did." Dayna looked away, feeling self-conscious under the gaze that seemed to be dissecting every word she spoke. "I suppose with you owning your own business it's best that men don't turn your head easily."

A frown furrowed her brow. "What does that mean?"

"Well," he answered with a shrug, "you'd never know if he was after your money or if he saw himself filling your shoes in the business when he gets you pregnant."

Dayna shot a look at him. "Only you would think that way."

"You mean," he taunted, "despite all that profound reasoning you do, you've never considered that possibility? Maybe that's what I want from you."

"No, you've been quite clear about what you want."

"Isn't it reassuring to know I'm one of the few men you can truly trust?" She looked away, holding back a smile and continuing to avoid his perceptive eyes as he asked, "You're not the least bit attracted to me, are you?"

Dayna hesitated before answering firmly, "No."

His fingers touched her chin and forced her to look at him. "You're lying." He leaned back against the porch and half-sat, half-stood against its edge. Even in the darkness surrounding them, she could feel his eyes sweeping over her disturbingly. "You don't seem to realize something about yourself, Dayna. Quibbling with you is like facing a stampede of cattle." Dayna couldn't hold back a burst of soft laughter. "It is," he insisted with a warm smile. "It's like facing danger and excitement at the same time. You break out in a cold sweat, your heart thunders in your chest. You want to run away, and yet something inside urges you to plunge forward to meet the risk. You have that effect on a man—on me," he added softly. "Your father wasn't so wrong when he called you a sweet witch. You're exasperatingly contradictory. You wanted to believe I saw pink tonight when you know I saw everything in a desirable shade of green."

Dayna smothered the smile his flattery provoked, remembering he was well-versed at saying all the right things when he wanted to. Brand continued, "I think you are a very intelligent, sensible, and level-headed lady. Maybe too sensible," he added. "Because I think that's the approach you use to everything, including the men in your life. You don't want to believe in romance. But for once, I think natural womanly emotions are overpowering all those convictions. That's why you're afraid of me, but it's also why you're with me now."

"I think I'll prove you wrong," she said confidently. She thought the rest would be easy, but as she made a move to leave him, he grabbed her wrist and she was drawn between his legs. His arm came around her waist as his powerful thighs locked around her limbs. The heat of his body mingled with hers, seeming to burn their clothes away. Dayna strained to free herself, pushing her hands against his chest, but the strength of his powerful body held her in an iron grip.

She sensed the futility of her struggle when his hand slid to the back of her head. His fingers entwined in her hair, stilling any further movement as he lowered his face toward hers with exquisite slowness. His mouth forced her lips to part, allowing his tongue to join the assault. There was a consuming, possessing quality to his kiss—gentle and tender, but forceful, demanding a passionate response. The warmth of his hand was like a scorching brand on her bare back as he molded her body against his. Her resistance melted away, all the pent-up emotions she had been battling burst out, and she slid her hands up his chest and around his neck. With a will of its own, her body leaned even closer into the warmth of his. No kiss from any man had ever made her tremble so she could hardly stand up. There seemed to be no end to the lingering, intoxicating kiss, and with every second that passed as his lips twisted and pressed against hers, she was drawn more and more to the man embracing her.

It was Brand who finally ended it. He lifted his head and loosened his embrace. Dayna swayed slightly, leaning against him again, unconsciously pressing her palm on his thigh to steady herself. She felt the muscles in his leg grow granite hard as they took her weight.

He drew in a quick breath, but his voice was calm when he spoke. "You're lying to yourself."

Confused by the desire still bubbling up in her from his forceful and commanding kiss, she tried to regain some hold on reality. With a suddenness that rocked her, she realized with dismay to what extent she had revealed her willingness to him. Her pride forced her to draw back her hand to slap him as an amused grin appeared on his face.

Lightning fast, Brand's hand encircled her wrist, arresting the stinging slap in midair. His fingers nearly crushed the bones of her wrist with their steely grip. "Are you that afraid?"

"I'm not afraid of you," Dayna countered. "Let me go!" Her heart was galloping, but she felt foolish and rushed her words. "I could have you fired for that."

His eyes taunted her. "I don't think so. You could hardly claim you weren't responsive." His gaze strayed to her breasts. The deep breaths she was taking testified to the excitement he had aroused in her.

"You won't tell anyone," Brand said as his hand slid possessively up her arm to the side of her neck. "We both know why you won't." Dayna's agitated breath became even more pronounced as Brand whispered, "Though you're trying to fight it, we both know this vacation is going to include more than you just basking in the sun."

Mischief danced in his blue eyes as he smiled confidently. It was the last thing she saw on his face before he left her and walked back toward the barbecue.

Leaning back against a pillar, she felt weak limbed and drained. Seconds passed before her breathing slowed and the stunned sensation suffusing her lifted. A culmination of emotions rushed through her as she made her way to her room. Shaken by what had just happened, she welcomed the solace and privacy of her room. She undressed quickly and slid beneath the sheet, hoping sleep would come quickly and drown the emotions Brand had stirred.

The lock on the door clicked and she squeezed her eyes shut, feigning sleep as Shelly and Karen entered the room. She lay perfectly still, hoping to avoid their barrage of questions. At the moment she had one question of her own to contemplate. Since Brand had made advances just as quickly to Alexandria Minter, she couldn't help wondering if he made a practice with any female guest who caught his fancy. It was a question that couldn't be answered tonight, but soon, Dayna thought, very soon, for her own good, she needed to know the answer.

Chapter Five

The following morning, after an old-fashioned country breakfast that Dayna sampled only lightly, she returned to her room and changed into riding clothes. She nodded approvingly at her reflection in the mirror. Clad in beige jeans, a long-sleeve green print cotton blouse, her new boots, and a recently purchased biscuit-colored Stetson, she walked toward the stables with Karen.

She liked to ride and had been looking forward to giving the Double R horses a good run. She smiled easily as Karen talked about the ranch. But Karen's casual remark about the weather slipped by her. Dayna's steps faltered. She tensed with apprehension; all her earlier cheerfulness was snatched away by the sight of Brand leaning casually against the stable doorway talking to Bonnie. Just as suddenly, Brand's conversation with Bonnie came to a halt. One brown finger pushed back the hat tilted low on his forehead. He raised his head and his eyes swept over her disturbingly.

She resisted an alien urge to run from him; then, to her relief, he entered the stables. Hiding her anxiety behind a bright, affable facade, she greeted Bonnie. "Good morning. We'd like to go riding."

Perched atop the corral fence, Bonnie jumped down and replied agreeably, "Sure can. Have you ridden before?"

"Oh, yes," Karen assured him. "We're weekend cowgirls from Chicago."

Bonnie gave a short laugh and Dayna was going to add a jest about her ability when Brand reappeared from the stable, the reins in his hand as he led two horses behind him.

Considering his manner the previous night, Dayna found the politeness in his voice annoyingly hypocritical. "Give the bay to Miss Palmer and the gray mare to Miss Hansen. And make sure they know how to saddle them, Bonnie."

Though his eyes were not on her, Dayna made a face at him. She wished she hadn't when she saw the mischievous light in his eyes. He had deliberately goaded her.

"I'm sure the ladies know how," Bonnie replied, glancing worriedly from Brand to Dayna. "You do, don't you?" he asked, nodding his head as if prodding them to give the right answer.

"Yes, we do," Karen answered.

Dayna remained silent, her mouth set in a thin, tight line as she shifted her attention to the horse. Bigger than Karen's, it was a beautiful animal with a dark brownish-red coat and a white, diamond-shaped mask. If she hadn't noted Bonnie's approving nod over Brand's choice, she would have been positive that the horse was an untamed monster, chosen to give her the ride of her life.

With a haughty lift of her chin, she turned to question Brand. Her eyes widened slightly with surprise. He was gone.

If his silent departure then was disturbing, the next few days were even more unnerving for just the opposite reason. It seemed that wherever Dayna went, Brand was nearby. The most impossible situation, however, was enduring his raking gaze at dinner time. Christy continued to monopolize his time, but whenever Dayna unwittingly glanced his way, she found she was the object of his interest.

A self-imposed isolation all Tuesday morning was more than she could stand. By afternoon, irritated with herself, she left her room. After all, she reminded herself, it was idiocy to waste time on a trip she wasn't enjoying.

Thoughts of finding Karen or Shelly were quickly discarded, as she realized she would be poor company in her present mood. In the lobby, she wandered over to the magazine rack. Perhaps a day of relaxation would lift her spirits. Idly, she leafed through a woman's magazine, but her interest wasn't held by the pages of fashionable clothes.

From lowered lids, she viewed W.R.'s office. Beside the highly polished oak desk in one of the soft leather chairs sat Brand. He swiveled the chair around and rested one arm on the desk. The temptation to eavesdrop was too strong. Dayna chided herself for it, but she remained stationed by the magazine rack as Brand gave W.R. his full attention. "I found another steer on the side of the road. Must have been hit by a diesel last night. I had to fire one man the other day because of his repeated negligence."

"You said they mended the open fence. So where are they getting out?"

Shaking his head slightly, Brand frowned. "I don't know. We've been checking into it for the past two days and found only that one break in the fencing. I assigned five men to ride different sections and look for another break. They all returned an hour ago saying it was locked tight." His gaze narrowed reflectively. "It makes me wonder how many are getting out that we don't know about. I think I'll go out myself." He shrugged but Dayna could see the frown firmly etched on his face. "We're not the only ranch with missing cattle. You know what that could mean."

"Big trouble."

Brand nodded. "The kind of trouble we need to end quick. Is there anything you want me to do before I start?"

"You mean for the guests?"

"Uh huh." Brand looked out at the lobby and Dayna quickly dropped her gaze to the magazine in her hand. "We've got a packed house. Are there a lot more coming between now and the middle of the week?"

"Not too many. Besides those who came a couple of days ago, there's a couple from California, and I think a few singles due to arrive tomorrow. And the Bensons. Remember them?"

A hint of laughter edged Brand's voice. "Two

youngsters, right? For their sake I hope they've outgrown switching the salt and sugar. Another prank like that and Charlie will chase them with his meat cleaver."

W.R. smiled. "There'll be about six more arriving next week. The three women who just arrived were last-minute accommodations, but for a friend, there's always a way to make room."

Brand made no comment on W.R.'s reference to his friendship with her father. "So that totals sixty, sixty-five guests. That's more than usual."

"It's the big vacation season right now, and we can easily accommodate them. I'm going to have Charlie make something special for dinner, and you make sure there are plenty of gentle horses for riding. I'm sure some instruction will be needed. We seem to have a rash of tenderfoots this year, so have someone down at the stables all the time who knows what to do."

Brand nodded and drew his long, lean body up. "If there's nothing else, I'm going down to the bunkhouse to talk to some of the hands. Maybe they've seen or heard something I haven't." With a wry smile, he added, "It seems that weekend in Phoenix was a mistake. Since I've been back all I've had are problems."

Dayna set one magazine back on the rack and picked up another as he started to turn toward the door, but W.R. stopped him. "Some of those problems are your own fault. What's all this about you and Miss Palmer?"

Dayna could suddenly feel Brand's eyes on her, but she heard his reply clearly. "She's just got a fiery spirit to match the color of her red hair."

"The lady's caught your eye?"

A soft masculine chuckle answered W.R. Dayna could see Brand's profile, with its soft lines crinkling from the corner of his eye. She just knew those disarming blue eyes were bright with humor. His voice confirmed her thought with its soft amused tone. "Definitely. Now *and* in Phoenix."

"That's what you meant when you said you'd met someone," W.R. said reflectively. "I can only assume the outcome of your last meeting didn't please you." Brand gave a noncommittal shrug, obviously unwilling to share too much of his personal life with his employer. "Even if that's the case," W.R. advised, "she is a guest. More important, she's a friend's daughter. I know," he said with a warning sound to his voice, "you never could resist the ones that needed taming, whether they were horses or women. Show a little caution, Brand. Just remember all the rough landings that go with it and make sure this doesn't get out of hand."

Brand reached for the doorknob. Even without looking up, Dayna knew his eyes were on her. "I'll remember. But—" he said confidently, "I always get what I want." Dayna growled mentally and quickly started toward the door of the lodge. He seemed so arrogant, she fumed, so sure of being victorious over any female that caught his fancy!

Meandering around the grounds, she strolled beyond the trees and shrubbery of the pool area. Set apart from the guest accommodations, which stood on hilly terrain, was the working ranch. It was as if she had stepped back in time. The original buildings, corrals, and stable had the look of the past. Overlooking all of it, on a nearby hill, was a great white farmhouse. Here was the working part of the cattle ranch, with the ranch hands' quarters, W.R.'s home, and the cookhouse. She strolled the area, stopping in the cookhouse, passing the horse stalls, and acknowledging the ranch hands' amiable greetings.

She wanted to see more, but the heat of the day was becoming uncomfortable. She'd decided to return to the air-conditioned lodge when she heard raucous shouts nearby. Curiously, she wandered in that direction instead. Staying hidden so she wouldn't be noticed by the ranch hands sitting and standing on a mesquite-log corral fence, she saw Brand inside the corral taking a rough, jostling, and bone-jarring ride, his body rocking atop a bucking mustang.

With something between fear and awe, she watched, expecting at any moment to see him plummet to the hard ground. Her heart pounded furiously until the animal gave in to his rider's tenacious efforts. Still showing some defiance to the authoritative hand controlling him, the horse circled the corral.

Dayna slipped away. Her breathing was quick, her heart still beating heavily. She blamed it on the fact that she was a city dweller viewing the rough side of ranching, but her mind refused to accept the lie. She couldn't ignore the frightened concern she felt for Brand.

As she reached the top of the hill and the main lodge building came into sight, Dayna saw Christy leaning against an ancient-looking buckboard, talking to one of the ranch hands, a man named John

Cutler. Dayna's fine brow arched with surprise. So Christy's interest included someone other than Brand. . . .

Walking down the small incline, Dayna stopped to see Bonnie, who was in the guest corral saddling a horse for one of the guests. Propping one elbow on the fence, she leaned her chin on her hand and watched in silence as his sun-weathered, worn-looking hands performed the task.

Bonnie glanced up, smiled, and then turned his attention back to the straps in his hands. "If Brand caught me doing this he'd chew me out for sure. He thinks if people come to a ranch they should do their own saddling and bridling. But lots of people aren't too good at it and I end up doing it for them anyway." He sent her another smiling glance. "You're pretty good at it."

"I'm a weekend equestrian. I try to get to the stables in the suburbs at least one weekend a month. My father can't ride at all," she said in an offhand manner. "It surprises me that W.R. and he have become such good friends, coming from such different worlds." Trying to maneuver the conversation toward one particular subject, she added, "It was nice they got together for a while in Dallas. Were you in charge of the guest ranch while W.R. was gone?"

"Most of the time it doesn't require a lot of work," Bonnie answered, indicating no self-importance. "Sara handles reservations and Charlie keeps everyone from starving. All I had to do was make sure the guests were kept happy. That's usually easy." Dayna was going to ask a more pointed question, but Bonnie changed the conversation before she had a chance. Drawing the cinch tighter, he shrugged. "You know, life's usually not too cluttered here. Everything is simple and honest. That's what I like about it. I guess it's a lot different from what you're used to."

Dayna nodded. "It is. I didn't really think I'd like it here, but I do. Everyone is very nice." Some people are too nice, she thought wryly.

"Are you looking forward to your first sight of a real live rodeo?"

Dayna laughed. "I never expected to say it, but yes, I am." She leaned back on the fence. "Do any of the wranglers here compete?"

"Sure," Bonnie answered, nodding his head.

"Is your foreman going to take part in the competition?" Bonnie's brows drew together in perplexity. Dayna was already biting her tongue, aware of how much she'd revealed, not just by her simple question but by the unnecessary sarcasm in her tone. She could never remember behaving so badly about anyone before. "I'm sorry, that really was uncalled for."

Bonnie shrugged a reply. "I understand. Sometimes a person just naturally gets under the skin of someone."

Bonnie had been easy to talk to from the very beginning, and Dayna admitted with a self-derisive laugh, "He just ruffles my feathers."

"Well, I can understand that too. He's stubborn and ornery. Always has been. Probably always will be. For the record, he's got enough trophies to line the wall of the fireplace in the lodge. He isn't

supposed to compete anymore. A Brahma got him
one time, hooked him with his horn, and made a
mighty fine rip." Dayna's brows knitted as Bonnie
explained, "He was told if he got hooked again like
that in the same place and more bone damage was
done, the best they could guarantee was a disabling
limp, maybe one leg not good for anything more
than to be dragged behind him." His shoulders
heaved with an exaggerated shrug. "But he's got a
stubborn streak in him that would equal a mule's,
and that itch is always there to be out riding with
the rest of those foolhardy cowpokes. Bull riding
gets into the system. Brand's no different than the
rest."

"But if it's dangerous, he shouldn't do it,"
Dayna said, not understanding why anyone would
tempt fate like that.

"He hasn't up until now. But he's the kind of
man who hankers for challenge. Being told not to
do something just makes him more bullheaded."
Dayna sensed that they were talking about more
than rodeo riding now; he was referring to Brand's
attitude toward her. Bonnie considered her another challenge in Brand's life and was offering her
advice about what to expect. He paused to deliberate what he was going to say; then he added, "You
two didn't start off on the right foot, I guess, and
sometimes Brand can be downright ornery, like I
said. He pushes and pushes until the other person
has to respond. Sometimes he's sweet as honey,
and other times he charges like a bull who's had a
red flag waved in front of him. He's just that way.
Won't back off from anything." Bonnie turned

toward her. "I suspect if there's a problem between you two, ma'am, it's because you're the same way—as strong-willed as he is."

"My," Dayna said lightly, "never did I expect to find a philosopher on a ranch."

"Me!" Bonnie snorted. "Little lady, I'm just telling you what's plain as the nose on your face. That don't take much hard thinking to see. I know you haven't asked me. And maybe I'm overstepping politeness," he added, "but I can't help myself from saying something else." He scratched his fingertips over the short stubble of whiskers already forming on the side of his jaw. "It seems to me that if avoiding him is going to make you unhappy as well as him, why keep fighting it?" His honest concern touched her. She smiled in response, feeling affection for the kindly man who was offering what he considered sound advice.

Bonnie chortled, "Might as well just relax and enjoy it. All that fighting and squealing don't do the calves any good when Brand wants to rope them. And, begging your pardon, ma'am, it's not that I'm comparing you to them, but," he said with a smile, "Brand usually gets what he wants."

Not this time, Dayna thought with a confident smile, placing her hand lightly on his arm in a thank-you gesture before she turned and headed for the lodge.

Through dinner that evening every effort Brand made to be alone with her was unwittingly thwarted by other guests, including Mrs. Whitaker, the schoolteacher and bird watcher. Dayna smiled with amusement, watching his expression alter from

polite endurance to exasperation as Mrs. Whitaker
offered a lengthy discourse on her favorite topic.
During the woman's dissertation about a purple
sandpiper she had studied during an Arctic trip,
Brand began to give up any hope of politely
maneuvering Dayna away from the woman. He left
with a shrug of resignation, although his blue eyes
met Dayna's for a brief second with a look of
impatient frustration.

It was close to ten the next morning when Dayna
finally descended the stairs to the lobby. Although
she had overslept the usual breakfast hour, she was
offered coffee and Danish pastry or toast. She
ordered only orange juice and coffee and read the
paper.

She returned to the room to find a note left by
Karen indicating that she and Shelly were at the
pool. Dayna changed into her swimsuit, thoughts
of a suntan paramount in her mind.

Deck furniture was scattered around the pool,
and Karen and Shelly were sitting on pastel lounge
chairs under the shade of a yellow-flowered pool
umbrella. Wearing a royal-blue maillot that
swooped low on her back to reveal a great amount
of bare skin at her waist and hips, Dayna laid her
towel on a chair and quickly donned a flowered
bathing cap. A few of the guests were already
enjoying the water, even though it was still morning. It was the beginning of March, and in many
other parts of the country people were still battling
the cold chill of winter. But even though in this
climate light jackets and sweaters might be re-

quired in the evening, Dayna had learned quickly how warm the weather could be during the day.

She dived into the pool, making a soft splash. After swimming a few laps she turned over and floated on her back to relax. The area around the pool was like some tropical island. A garden of lush desert plants, pink- and white-flowered oleander bushes, palm trees, and wispy Palo Verde trees encompassed the area, making it a paradise of cool greenery.

Drops of water trailed her as she climbed from the pool, her body glistening in the sunlight. Removing the cap, she gave a quick shake of her head and stretched out on one of the lime-colored lounge chairs. Karen handed her the bottle of suntan lotion she had brought along. Dayna became absorbed in smoothing the liquid over her arm and shoulder as Karen commented, "Christy was really working diligently at pursuing Brand again last night." Dayna visualized the winks being exchanged between her friends. She looked up, knowing Karen would continue until she offered some kind of response.

"No comment," Dayna answered with a smile.

"Have you made any deductions about him yet regarding Alexandria Minter?"

Applying lotion to her leg, Dayna shrugged, but a nagging thought slipped out. "If you promise not to make some snide remark, I'll tell you what really bothers me. From personal experience, I just don't think he'd force himself on a woman."

Karen questioned excitedly, "He did make a pass at you, didn't he?"

"I told you what happened in Phoenix. He's even more determined now to prove he's a master at seduction. But," she said thoughtfully, "I've always felt he was letting me set the pace. He said as much."

"So?" Karen queried. "Are you going to let him provide you with some extra activity?"

Dayna didn't comment. Giving her friend an amused look along with a shake of her head, she smoothed lotion over her other leg. As the conversation changed to a discussion of Martin Randolph, Dayna looked up, squinting to see how large a cloud was shading her as a sudden shadow blocked the sun. She viewed instead an extremely masculine body standing over her.

"I have to go to town for supplies," Brand said, "and I thought one of you might like to keep me company and see some of the local sights." His quiet assurance implied he'd already chosen his companion.

Karen and Shelly looked at each other, their silence indicating that they, too, were aware of whom he wanted to join him. Though her eyes were lowered, Dayna could feel the heat of his gaze as he sat down on the lounge chair closest to her.

He watched her as she carefully concentrated on spreading lotion along a slender limb. "Wouldn't you like to do something more exciting?" His voice was suggestive. "I could give you a preview ride of the Indy 500."

His words brought soft laughter from Karen and Shelly. Facing the problem at hand, Dayna responded, "I'm busy."

"So I see," he replied with a hint of humor in his eyes as they followed her hand's movement over her thigh. "I think you're afraid to be with me."

"Would you stop saying that?"

Laughter filled his voice. "Why do you pretend? I know you stood around yesterday watching me."

Dayna's whole body burned with embarrassment. She had no words of defense to utter. The glint in his blue eyes was more unsettling than the ensuing silence.

"Come with me," he persisted in a soft, coaxing voice. "Prove you're not afraid."

His challenge was unavoidable. She tried to calm the odd emotion sweeping through her. Never had she given in to any man. She certainly wouldn't let *him* get the better of her. Her proud confidence aroused, she rose to her feet, feeling a strong need to be in a position to stare down at his goading expression. It wasn't quite so easy to appear in control with his eyes following her body's movement and appraising lingeringly the bare skin revealed by her swimsuit. Dayna took up Brand's challenge. "All right. I'll prove it. I'll meet you outside the lodge in ten minutes," she added, before turning away from him.

For all her bravado, she was shaking and weak limbed from the raw desire in his gaze as it perused her bare legs and hips. Her hands shook visibly as she changed into jeans and began buttoning her blouse. Muttering a curse under her breath, she sat down on the edge of the bed and took a brief moment to try to control the emotions she had been struggling with ever since they met.

Dayna jumped, surprised when the door opened and Karen entered. "I came up for some magazines."

Not wanting Karen to see the emotional turmoil she was in, Dayna looked down and worked on another button of her blouse.

"Are you going?" Karen asked, jumping herself when a second later there was a soft rap on the door.

Dayna grabbed at her blouse, holding it together as Karen answered the knock. After a murmured exchange, she turned back to Dayna. "Hank, the ranch hand," she explained, "just came to tell me about a wilderness survival program they're offering." Dayna nodded, relieved her hands were steadier now as Karen went on. "I asked down at the desk this morning about it. Might as well try everything as long as I'm here," she added.

"It was nice of him to make a special trip to let you know."

"They're all nice here," Karen noted. "Are you having similar thoughts about trying everything as long as you're here?" Dayna released an exasperated sigh and Karen quickly continued. "Look, I've never seen you act like this with any man before. Usually you seem so sure of yourself, so much in control."

Pulling on her boots, Dayna shook her head. "Karen, what you saw was my own fault for being vulnerable and reacting like any other woman to a man who's well versed in making a woman pay attention to him." A sly smile curled her mouth. "That cowboy needs to be put in his place. He thinks all he has to do is snap his fingers and every woman in sight will fall at his feet," she added, still fuming over his challenge. "If I was interested in wasting my time I might just play a little game with that ranch foreman and give him a taste of his own medicine."

"Is that why you're going with him?" Karen asked.

Dayna shook her head. "No. . . ." She had no real answer. Why was she going? She ran a brush over her hair and hoped Karen wouldn't ask any more probing questions.

"Are you going to confront him about Alexandria Minter?"

"I'm not really sure. I don't have any positive proof. If I did ask him, it might just give him a chance to counter the complaint with some story."

"Do you really believe he's that devious?"

"Karen, his job could be in jeopardy. He might lie through his teeth to keep it."

The motor of the blue pickup was running, and Brand was waiting patiently in the driver's seat, a complacent smile crinkling the lines at the corners of his eyes.

Dayna passed Hank, nearly bumping into him as he finished a conversation with Brand and yelled back, "I'll tell Bonnie you're getting it from town now."

She sidestepped him and smiled, drawing an apologetic look from Hank. Tipping his hat, he smiled. "Sorry, ma'am."

She laughed as she hurried around the front of the pickup truck. "Ma'am" seemed to be the polite greeting for any woman, whether single, married, twenty, or eighty. She had been called that at least fifty times since she'd arrived. As soon as she closed the door, Brand pulled the truck away from the ranch, leaving clouds of dust on the road behind them. Knowing he had artfully intimidated her with his dare to accompany him, her voice betrayed her annoyance. "Do you always go around challenging the guests?"

He turned to look at her for a second and then his eyes slid back to the road. "It seemed the only way to get you to come with me. You've been very shrewdly avoiding me for the last few days. I am trying to be nice and offer to show you some of the sights around the ranch that not many of the guests see."

"Preferential treatment?"

"You'd be my first choice every time."

"Do you always give special attention to certain guests?"

"You are a very special lady," he said quietly.

"How many other special ladies have you known?" Dayna persisted.

His blue eyes narrowed, but they held steady on the road. "What are you really asking?"

Dayna kept her eyes on the passing scenery. "It was just curiosity." With his continued silence, she added, "I wondered if you made a habit of taking female guests to town."

He didn't answer her question directly. "Since you're with the travel agency, it would be logical to want to impress you, wouldn't it?"

He negotiated a curve. Sunlight glared into his eyes and he squinted against it. While he drove she studied the strong features of his face. It was virile and rugged, yet he had eyes that could be both boyishly mischievous and alarmingly sensuous. Her eyes lingered on the well-sculptured cheekbones, the firm jawline, the long, straight nose.

The sun no longer posed a problem and Brand turned an interested glance in her direction. "Surely, you know that isn't why I really asked you along."

"I'm a little surprised employees are allowed such freedom with guests."

A corner of his mouth curled. "I'd like a lot more with you."

"W.R. doesn't mind you associating with female guests?"

His mouth slanted in a smile. "I associate with all the guests. Earlier this morning I took a ten-year-old out to rope a calf."

"Yes, but you do target women mostly for your attention," she persisted. "It's true, isn't it, that you've had brief romances with other women?"

"Some not so brief."

"I mean with guests. I'm not the first," Dayna asked, "am I?" The questions popped out without thinking.

"Are we going to have a romantic interlude?" Brand asked with a grin. "It's nice to finally hear you admit it."

Dayna clamped her lips together and stared out the window. She was getting no answers this way.

Discerning her stubborn silence, he said easily, "Look, there isn't any harm in a romance to enjoy, to make the most of, if both people face it honestly." He laughed shortly. "In this day, it's hardly shocking for a man to tell a woman he wants to make love to her." Dayna's head turned in his direction. "I assume someone who is sophisticated and beautiful, and who has traveled extensively, has received many propositions."

"Of course, but do you think I go around having casual flings with men?"

"I don't know. But I assure you the word 'casual' has no place in describing what I feel for you. I've hardly hidden from you what I want, and I think you want me."

Dayna knew he was trying to lighten her mood but a frown had settled on her face. She swallowed hard. Had he actually stated that all he wanted was a two-week affair?

Preoccupied with driving, he glanced in his rear-view mirror and negotiated a turn on to the state highway. A few minutes passed before he commented without looking at her, "We'll play the game a while longer, Dayna."

"Game?" Dayna questioned softly, a strange ache beginning to swell in her chest as she said the word.

"That's what it is," Brand answered. "You're only fighting yourself."

Dayna offered no reply, returning her attention to the passing scenery. She was almost afraid to think too deeply about anything. She felt it was more important to give herself breathing space, to take her time and contemplate everything he'd said, but it didn't stop her from asking a personal question. "Did you ever meet anyone you were serious about?"

Brand shook his head. "No, I was young but smart enough to see I would grow tired of the relationship when the initial excitement in bed disappeared."

"You think that's all there is to a relationship, don't you?"

"No, but it certainly keeps the romance alive."

"Romance, excitement in bed," she said with a cynical air. "Those are the only important things to men like you."

Brand cast a curious glance at her. "What kind of man do you think I am?" he asked with a hint of laughter.

"A womanizer, a man who enjoys women for the conquest. One who lives his life having casual flings," Dayna answered bluntly.

He didn't react as Dayna had anticipated. Soft laughter rumbled in his throat. "You came up with all those reasonable deductions because I said I grew tired after the initial excitement disappeared? You certainly don't look the naive type." He was quiet for a moment. "What do you think *is* important?"

"Common interests, mature views, a good foundation," she explained. "And you've admitted you've never been serious about any of them. So much for romance. It's an empty gesture."

"There was one," he said with a quiet softness. "I met her at college." He seemed to drift away for a minute, as if recapturing a memory.

"You went to college? Did you work your way through?"

"Part of the time," he answered, his voice stronger, indicating his mind was with her again. "I started out majoring in forestry and got sidetracked into computer technology."

Dayna returned his smile. "Which explains your fascination with the computer system they were using for the rodeo."

Brand answered with a self-deprecating expression. "I was drifting in those days. Not sure what I wanted. After I struggled for the first two years, living on beans and junk food every night, my father came to me and said: 'Well, you've proven yourself to me, I'll pay the rest of the way.'"

Thoroughly enjoying the thought that someone had gotten the best of him, Dayna wanted to smile but responded instead with an understanding remark. "What a stinker."

Brand laughed. "I thought so at the time. I'm sure he enjoyed himself over it. But it was good for me. I really wasn't acting too responsibly, and I guess he thought I wouldn't finish college. It's funny how easy it is to say that now. Back then I really couldn't understand how he could be so uncooperative. He'd worked hard all his life, though, and he probably didn't think I should have anything handed to me."

"How did he feel about you going back to ranching after all that education?"

Brand shrugged. "I think he sensed I would all along. I was raised out in this country. I like it. Everything always came easily to me on the ranch." He added wryly, "Born in the saddle, as they say." He cast a sidelong glance at her. "You figured," he said thoughtfully, "with no education, I was doing the only thing I'm capable of doing. Right?"

Dayna quickly denied this. "No. In fact, when I saw you in Phoenix I thought you were there on business for some eastern company. I just don't understand why you came back to ranching."

"That's easy to answer," Brand said firmly. "I told you already. I like it. It's what I wanted."

Dayna looked up, only becoming aware they were in town when Brand halted the truck for a stop sign. As he pulled it into a diagonal parking space, he added, "I don't give up easily. I usually get what I want."

She slammed the door behind her and hurried to meet him in front of the truck. Dayna was irritated when she saw the glint of amusement that always seemed to be in his eyes when he looked at her.

They had parked in front of an old-fashioned general store. As she walked beside him up the wooden steps, Dayna suddenly became conscious of the power and strength in his body. Never had she considered her own stature as slight. She had dated many men over six feet tall but there was a compelling physical quality about Brand she couldn't ignore as they walked under the porch awnings.

For the sake of the tourists the local storekeepers had worked hard to maintain the authenticity of an old frontier town, complete with hitching posts along the streets in front of the shops. The only suggestion of modern civilization in the main section of town were the typical street-corner gas stations. For a city girl, it was an interesting sight.

While Brand made small talk with the shop owner, Dayna stood back and viewed the establishment. Reminiscent of a frontier store, it contained shelf-lined walls laden with every item a customer could ever want. Along with an old-fashioned meat scale and a paper and string dispenser for packages, there were rolls of fabrics off to one corner. On the counter before her were glass containers filled with various candies: peppermint and cinnamon sticks, gum drops and spice drop slices.

They made two more stops for supplies. Not interested in the hardware store he had to visit, she left him and wandered along the street, taking in the sights. When he found her browsing over postcards, Dayna noticed the supplies were already in the truck. She assumed he was ready to return to the ranch, but without a word of explanation, he grabbed her hand and led her toward what appeared to be a frontier saloon. Before Dayna could utter a word they were inside, not a tavern, but the ice cream parlor next door.

Dayna noted the care that had been given to the decor to create an authentic Gay Nineties atmosphere. As Brand seated her in one of the white wrought-iron chairs with its peppermint-striped cushioned seat, it seemed ridiculous to protest something as innocent as an ice cream soda. "Ice cream sodas and cowboys seem out of context. Aren't you more inclined toward beer?" she taunted.

His smile slipped away, the blue eyes narrowing and becoming undecipherable. "I see your opinion about cowboys remains the same as when we first met."

It really hadn't. Since she had been at the ranch and met such fine people as W.R. and Bonnie and

so many other wranglers, she'd given up her nega-
tive opinion of cowboys, but she needed some kind
of protection. And though it was a feeble defense
against Brand's overpowering personality, she
thought her sarcasm might help her to sidestep any
future romantic notions.

"Is that the real problem?" Brand continued as
blunt as ever. "You've got something against jeans
and cowboy boots?"

"No, of course not," Dayna answered, disturbed
that she felt so defensive.

"That's good," he grinned, seemingly completely unaffected by her previous comment, "because,
lady, you look great wearing them."

His blue eyes sparkled at her mockingly. Dayna
quickly looked down, knowing she had meant her
earlier words to provoke him and make him angry.
Instead, the opposite seemed to have happened.
She was fighting embarrassment while he was sitting back in the chair looking thoroughly amused.

A teenager wearing a white jacket and straw hat
arrived bearing two enormous chocolate sodas,
heavily laden with whipped cream and nuts. Dayna
listened with interest as he asked Brand some
questions about the upcoming rodeo and then
shared a private joke about a bull named Gentle
Ride.

Brand still wore an indulgent smile as the boy
walked away. He commented matter-of-factly,
"He's been entering bronc-riding competitions up
until now and thinks he's ready for the big time."

"Bull riding?"

"Uh huh." He laughed and pushed his hat back
to a cocky angle on his head. "I was the same way

at his age. The old 'I've-got-to-prove-I'm-a-man'
syndrome."

"I heard about the accident with the bull."

"From Bonnie, no doubt. It's no big deal."

Still nettled over her previous embarrassment,
she gave in to an impish impulse and baited him
without thinking. "I suppose it takes a lot of
courage to do it after you've been hurt."

A gaze as cold as ice was turned on her. "What
are you saying? I don't have it?"

The underlying anger in his voice made her
aware that her gibe had touched him. The conse-
quences of her snide remark suddenly became
more important to her than anything else. "No,"
she answered, vigorously shaking her head. Worried that he was truly offended and would take her
words as a challenge, she added quickly, "I didn't
mean that the way it sounded." But his handsome
features were still tense, and Dayna tried to undo
what she thoughtlessly might have started. "You
were badly hurt. It would be foolish to compete
again."

His head tilted slightly, questioningly, and his
gaze softened at the concern he heard in her voice.
She was much too sensitive to be sarcastic with
someone, he thought. Her tender heart would
always make her vulnerable. His eyes glinted with
mischievous lights. "I might get another scar if I
compete. They make nice battle wounds and gain
attention," he said with a grin, offering Dayna the
cherry from his soda. "Some women find a hidden
scar sexy."

Dayna gave a noncommittal shrug and directed
her attention to spooning the ice cream from her

soda. "No one can see the one you've got now, can they? It's on your leg."

His blond brow arched in response, making Dayna aware she'd said too much. His smile could only be interpreted as devilish as he ran his fingers along the upper part of his inner thigh and partially into his groin. "It's right here."

"Oh." As Dayna's eyes followed his hand's movement, the color rose to her face. It was quite clear that the only way anyone would see his so-called battle wound was if he was naked. Her face crimsoned even more, and she wondered with a frown how he had managed to turn the tables on her again.

Quickly she changed the subject, hoping as she gestured with her spoon toward the soda he wouldn't tease her about the blush. "This is very good." Brand's eyes were fixed on her, the deep, contemplative look daring her to look back at him. Not willing to meet his gaze, she concentrated on the nostalgic decor and hoped he'd say something to end the nervous one-sided conversation she was engaging in. "It's really marvelous the way they've made it so authentic."

His voice was soft. "I like what I see."

She asked, "Are you going to persist in staring at me?"

He leaned toward her, a smile accompanying his words. "It would be harder not to. You are a beautiful woman."

The long-handled spoon slipped from her fingers and his larger hand captured hers, forcing Dayna to raise her eyes to him. Damn, she thought with irritation, why does he have to be so gentle?

"You're very beautiful. And smart. And a little shrewd," he added, squinting slightly.

The soothing, caressing sound of his voice quickened her pulse. Dayna couldn't prevent the pink blush of self-conscious embarrassment from sweeping over her cheeks.

His hand squeezed hers affectionately. "You're also really kind of sweet."

"You have an overzealous imagination," she said, calling on all the poise her twenty-seven years could command.

Mocking lights glinted in his eyes but his voice was low and husky. "You're right about that. I've been fantasizing about you since the first moment we met. This is much nicer. I'm glad we're not at each other's throats."

"I think you're a little too smooth for me."

His amused chuckle answered her. "I doubt it. I'm the country boy, remember? You're the sophisticated one from the big city." He released her hand and said quite seriously, "Actually, you call the shots, Dayna. If you don't like the direction you're going, you can change it. I like being with you." He shrugged one shoulder and appeared to laugh at himself. "Even when we're sparring."

He looked down at his soda, and Dayna's eyes narrowed skeptically. She doubted very much that he meant what he had just said. He assumed he was in control and just as definitely had already determined where they were headed.

Most of the trip back was spent in silence. Brand turned the truck onto the dirt road that led to the ranch and stepped on the gas as they approached the building. The speed of the truck reminded her of her first day there and his abrupt welcome. Some instinct made her caution him. "You'd better slow down. What if W.R. sees you speeding again?"

A crease formed between Brand's brows, but he quickly complied with her warning and slowed the truck to a respectable speed. Dayna noticed his amused smile, and she was confused by her own actions. What did she care if he got into trouble with W.R.? Wasn't that exactly where she would put him eventually if Alexandria Minter's story was true? Despite such realistic, disturbing thoughts, she was relieved she had warned him when she saw W.R. emerge from the lodge as they approached.

"Did you get all the supplies?" he asked, walking over to the truck when they stopped. When Brand nodded affirmatively, W.R. advised, "Well, if I were you I'd hightail them over to Charlie before he comes chasing after you with that meat cleaver of his."

Dayna was ready to punch Brand. He was offering no explanation, and she wondered anxiously if W.R. might be getting the wrong impression about their late return as he added, "He said you left for town early this morning and he expected you back hours ago. He needs some of the supplies for tonight's dinner."

"We were a little detained. I'll take Dayna with me. A smile from her in Charlie's direction should protect me from Chinese torture."

W.R. cast an anxious look in her direction. Vividly, she recalled his conversation with Brand concerning her. Did W.R. think she needed words of warning too? If he did, his anxiety equaled hers. "You'd better hurry," he stated before turning back toward the lodge.

When they reached the side of the main building where the kitchen was located, Dayna made a move to open her door and help him. But he was out of the truck and approaching the steps with the two boxes in his arms before she even stirred into action. An irate Charlie, wearing a mandarin-collared shirt and dark sack pants, met him in the doorway. Although Charlie came only as high as Brand's chin, he acted as if he was equal in strength and height to the man standing before him with arms encumbered. Charlie's thin mustache twitched violently as he berated Brand for taking so long.

Only a few short sentences from Brand and Charlie, quiet now, looked over Brand's shoulder and eyed her. With a bowing smile to her, Charlie accepted the two boxes and went back in the kitchen.

Shoving his hat back to a casual position on his head, Brand flashed a reckless smile at her. It completed the carefree picture he presented. She realized then that she liked his smile, she liked the sound of his voice—in fact, she liked everything about him.

A struggle was beginning inside her. They hardly knew each other. And after all the men she'd met who had shown the same smooth actions and had spoken similar sweet words, how could she be falling for him so easily? she wondered with a slight frown.

She waited until he was seated next to her again to ask, "Was Charlie angry?"

"Only briefly."

"I thought you wanted my help?"

His hand rested on her thigh. "No, I knew I could handle him, but this way I kept you with me a little longer."

His blue eyes met hers. They caressed her face intimately before his gaze settled on her lips; it was obvious he was thinking of kissing her again. Dayna fought the temptation to let it happen as the beat of her heart quickened. The magnetic power he possessed commanded her to lean toward him, and her body swayed slightly in his direction before she found the will to break free and quickly open the truck door.

As she slammed it shut and turned toward the lodge, she yelled out, "See you."

Despite the carefree manner of her departure, her voice was charged with emotion. Was she really starting to feel something for him? It was ridiculous.

Inside their room, Karen and Shelly were in various stages of dressing in preparation for dinner. Judging from the pink color of Shelly's nose, Dayna guessed they both had stayed by the pool too long. Karen moved her shoulders slowly as if in agony—her skin was taut and red.

Dayna asked the obvious. "Sunburned?"

"Hmmm," Karen groaned. "You were gone a long time," she said, reaching for the first-aid cream in her flight bag.

Dayna reached out for the tube. "Here, turn around. I'll do your back." Lightly smoothing the cream over the bright pink flesh of Karen's shoulders, Dayna asked, "Why didn't you come inside sooner?"

Karen winced as Dayna touched a tender spot. "Dumb." She looked back over her shoulder at Dayna. "Did you have fun today?"

Putting the cap back on the tube of cream and handing it to Karen, Dayna sat down on her bed and began to remove her boots. Absently, she answered, "Brand showed me the town and some historical landmarks."

Lying carefully down on the bed, Karen eyed Dayna. Despite the indifference Dayna tried to convey for the man she had spent the whole afternoon with, it was apparent there was a new lift to her spirits.

Dayna caught the meaningful look on Karen's face and released an exasperated sigh. She didn't need Karen to say out loud what she was battling to suppress. Brand had stirred new emotions in her. It was that revelation more than anything that really bothered her. She wasn't a fool. And yet even forewarned about the kind of man he was, she seemed unable to suppress the feelings he aroused so effortlessly.

With a few minutes to spare before dinner, Dayna wrote a quick letter to her father, informing him that she hadn't learned anything *yet*.

Chapter Six

$\mathcal{D}$ayna stood at the floor-to-ceiling window in the lobby and watched a rising sun break above the mountains. Normally a morning groaner who hated to wake before ten, since she had arrived at the ranch she had made a point of getting up early just to see the marvelous sunrises. There usually wasn't a great deal of activity that early in the morning; however this morning was different. Upon entering the lobby she had found new guests arriving and others who were ending their stay, preparing for their transportation to the airport by Bonnie.

W.R. was in his office with a man she had never met. She assumed he was a new guest, a businessman. She would have given no more thought to him, but as she turned to enter the dining room for breakfast, W.R. came out of the office with the man and proceeded in her direction. The stranger

was almost as tall as W.R., trim and conservative
in appearance, and Dayna noted there was a vague
similarity in appearance between the two men.

W.R. stopped her and asked, "Have you seen
Brand, Dayna?"

That simple question made it clear that her name
had been linked with Brand's through the wranglers' grapevine, which, Dayna had already
learned, relayed news faster than any group of
office gossips. With some annoyance, she wondered just who was spreading stories about her and
Brand. It was easy to guess. Even though Dayna
had managed to keep some distance between
Brand and her, she had no doubt a few stories had
been exaggerated, including one describing her
relatively compliant attitude when they were in
Phoenix. There was no other explanation for
W.R.'s assumption that she would know where
Brand was. She veiled her indignation and answered him with a shake of the head. "No."

"Have you seen him at all this morning?"

Dayna shifted on her feet, discomfited even
more by the cool scrutiny of W.R.'s companion.
His assessment, though not as bold or sensuous as
Brand's, was still unnerving. It was as if he were
trying to analyze her inner self. Already having
guessed that the man before her was W.R.'s son,
she wondered just what had been said about her to
provoke such a curious regard. "No, I haven't."
She glanced at Bonnie, who had just entered the
lobby and was standing in the doorway.

Her look was caught by W.R., who looked over
his shoulder and growled at Bonnie, "Do you know
where he's gone?"

"Sir?" Bonnie asked in bafflement.

W.R.'s voice was filled with impatience as he shot one word at Bonnie. "Brand."

Ambling over to them, Bonnie shook his head. "Not now. Last time I saw him was right about dawn. He was riding Valiant in the direction of the river."

W.R.'s brow cleared. "Oh, yes, that's right. He was supposed to exercise the horse. It's been acting cagey the last couple of days. A high-spirited animal gets rambunctious if it isn't ridden regularly."

The man next to W.R. cleared his throat, and W.R.'s face lit up with a proud smile. He directed his smile at Dayna. "I'm sorry, Dayna. That darn Brand and his disappearing act has me so up in arms I forgot my manners." Placing an arm around the shoulder of the younger man beside him, W.R. said, "This is my son, Tom, Dayna. Thomas, Dayna Palmer." As the man shook Dayna's hand, W.R. continued. "He's visiting for a few days. Although he's here on business, I think he's looking to stretch his muscles—they get cramped up from sitting day after day behind a desk."

Responding to his father with an indulgent smile, Tom Reardon laughed easily and said, "My pleasure, Miss Palmer. Don't believe him. I feel just as cramped up after I get off a horse." He looked at her politely but with interest. "She is as beautiful a woman as you were telling me. You certainly didn't exaggerate."

Dayna's friendly smile was replaced by a quizzical frown, as she wondered why W.R. would discuss her. Quickly he explained, a furrowed brow indicating his embarrassment over his son's state-ment, "I was telling Tom there was more beautiful scenery inside the lodge than out this year, and I happened to mention your name, Dayna. I hope you're not offended."

Dayna smiled. "No, of course not. I'm flattered. Thank you for the compliment."

Appearing relieved, W.R. said, "If you'll excuse us, Dayna, we have some business to discuss. I'm beginning to believe attorneys are like doctors—always working." He winked. "I'll humor Tom now and maybe he'll sit and relax with me later."

It was apparent Tom's opinion of her was favor-able, and he said warmly, "Nice meeting you, Miss Palmer."

"I'm sure we'll see each other again over the next few days. Please call me Dayna."

Tom nodded his head, acknowledging her prefer-ence for informality, and with his father headed for the office. As W.R. reached the door, he glanced back at Bonnie. "See if you can find Brand. Tom wants to talk to him." In a softer tone but one still edged with irritation, W.R. requested, "Dayna, if you do see Brand, would you inform him I want to see him immediately?"

Dayna nodded her head in answer. From the irritation she heard in W.R.'s voice, if Brand knew what was good for him, he'd better show up somewhere soon.

That morning she took a trip around the ranch, even going so far as to ask one of the ranch hands if he had seen Brand, but her search was to no avail; he couldn't be found.

By midafternoon it was becoming a driving obsession to find him and confront him with her suspicion that he was allowing the ranch hands to believe she was already just another female on his long list of conquests. Spotting his chestnut quarter horse tied outside one of the sheds, she stormed in that direction.

Word must have circulated that Dayna was searching for Brand because one ranch hand coming toward her deliberately altered his course and took the long way around the corral to the lodge just to avoid meeting her. She nearly whirled around and returned to the lodge, as it occurred to her that, by seeking him out, she might be fueling the stories already started. Why was it that every other day he had seemed to be underfoot constantly and today he had managed a prize-winning disappearing act?

Flinging open the shed door, Dayna assumed a battle stance, while her eyes bore into the broad back of the man standing before her. She cleared her throat loudly. When he began to turn around, Dayna opened her mouth to berate Brand for what she was now sure was an intentional game of hide-and-seek. Swiftly she clamped her lips together as she spotted a stranger's face.

Offering Dayna a surprised smile, he said, "Hi, there, can I help you?"

At a loss, Dayna stood like an empty-headed ninny. She cringed mentally, visualizing the fool she had almost made of herself and the laugh the ranch hands would have had over such an asinine display on her part.

She gave a clipped reply to his question. "No, I—I was just looking around."

He nodded politely, but his grin clearly declared that he knew whom she was looking for. Smiling briefly at him, Dayna hurried out the shed door. She shook her head, dismayed at the obsessive need she had had to find Brand. Dismally, she wondered what her real motive had been. And now she had nearly made a laughing stock of herself because of it. Never before had she acted so ridiculously about a man. Mentally she scolded herself. No more! In anger, she stomped off up the hill toward the lodge.

She stopped abruptly as Bonnie stuck his head out of a nearby barn door. "Ma'am, Brand's here. He'd like to see you."

Dayna reeled around, hurrying toward the barn, passing Bonnie on the way. His knowing smile made Dayna question her own actions. Just why did she want to see Brand so badly? As she reached the barn door, she assured herself it was to have it out with him and stop not only his pursuit of her but any falsehoods he might be tempted to spread about their relationship. With that purpose in mind, she flung open the barn door.

Inside she was met by a strong aroma of horse and hay. A glance down the aisle to the individual stalls showed no sign of Brand. A quick look behind and above her toward the loft also gave no clue to his whereabouts. She was about ready to leave, find Roscoe T. Bonner, and reprimand him for his not-so-funny sense of humor when she heard Brand's deep, soothing voice. "There— almost done."

Dayna followed the sound. In the last stall she found him hunkered down, scrutinizing the white stallion's hoof. She stood in silence, leaning against one of the barn uprights and watching the strength in his sun-browned hands as they held the horse's hoof steady. She thought she hadn't made a sound, but Brand's head snapped around in her direction. "I didn't know you were here." Pulling a rag from his pocket, he wiped his hands. "When did you come in?"

Dayna offered a brittle smile in response to the latest deception. "Right after you asked me to come."

A crease formed between his fair brows. "When was that?"

Dayna moved forward. This ridiculous act of innocence rankled her. "Did you or did you not ask Bonnie to tell me you wanted to see me?"

His eyes fastened on her face. He stared at her uncomprehendingly at first, and then answered with laughter in his voice, "Why, that old codger." He shook his head and didn't need to say more.

Wishing the floor would cave in, Dayna was at a loss as to what to say. Brand's smile didn't help. He knew she had come running the minute she thought he wanted to see her. She spun around to beat a hasty retreat, sure that Brand probably knew also of her determined efforts all day to find him.

There was no point in trying to explain her reasons. Squaring her shoulders, she moved rapidly down the aisle, not wanting him to see her face turn crimson with humiliation. She yanked at the barn door, but an outstretched arm closed it. Dayna stared at the hand barring her exit. Brand's breath caused strands of her hair to flutter and his mouth was so close it tickled her ear, sending a shiver of anticipation through her. "Don't go, Dayna. I'm glad you're here." His lips lightly touched the side of her neck and gently caressed her earlobe. Unwittingly she swayed back against him as his hands touched her shoulders and his mouth moved with light, disturbing kisses over the base of her neck and upper shoulder. She could feel desire kindling in him when his hand moved to her waist and pressed her back against the hardness of his body.

Effortlessly, he turned her to face him and his arms tightened around her back.

"I am teasing, but you deserve it," he said, kissing the tip of her nose. "You torment me unmercifully with your game playing."

"I haven't been playing any games," Dayna answered, meeting warm eyes. As his hand slowly moved down her spine to the rounded edge of her buttocks, she knew she had made a mistake in seeking him out, in being alone with him now.

"Why are you pretending you came only because Bonnie told you I wanted to see you, when we both know you've been looking for me all day?"

Color dotted her cheeks and she tried to pull free, but the masculine hands on her back intensified their pressure to keep her close. She rushed into an explanation that seemed ridiculous now as she stood in his embrace. "I had a few things I wanted to say to you."

His voice was filled with humor. "Do you have to act typically female now? You don't really want to talk."

"Yes, I do," Dayna countered with a frown. "What do you mean, typically female?"

"Hard to get," Brand answered easily, bending his head and nibbling lightly on her earlobe.

Dayna closed her eyes in response. It was costing her a great effort to think clearly. "Men," she started and then paused, forgetting what she was going to say as his lips followed the dainty contour of her ear. She gave her head a slight shake and pulled away from his mouth. "Men always think that when they don't get their own way," she managed to say with a steadiness she wasn't feeling.

"What would you call it?" he queried, his tongue caressing her neck with a feather-light stroke.

"Women aren't as casual about sex. And that's what I want to talk to you about," she said quickly, pressing her hands against his chest. It didn't really separate his body from hers, but it did stop his affectionate assault on her neck.

"I'd prefer to think of it as making love," he said lightly, completely ignoring her reproachful tone.

"Love is not what some men are thinking about," Dayna answered, lowering her gaze and focusing on his smiling mouth. She worked hard to repress her natural feminine instincts, which were aroused just by the sight of his lazy, almost insolent, smile.

"That's true of some women, too," Brand said in answer to her last comment. The hand that had been resting lightly on her back moved to the curve of her slender neck. His eyes shifted to the strands of silky, copper-colored tresses sliding through his fingers as he played with her soft-textured hair. He twined the mass of it around his hand, and Dayna felt the firm pressure of his palm on the back of her head, where it held her face still beneath his gaze. "What about you, Dayna?" he asked with husky softness.

"I think," she managed, "you'd just better let me go. You assume too much. And," she added, drawing a deep, calming breath, "I think you've been allowing other people to assume too much about us."

"No, I haven't. But maybe you have. You're the one who's been looking all day for me. Remember?"

Dayna bristled beneath the mockery in his eyes. "I just told you why I was looking for you."

"Sounds good," he answered with a taunting smile.

"You're not really listening, are you?"

"Sure I am. But I'm also a patient man, Dayna. And when something is inevitable, I'll wait for it."

Dayna was given no space or time to hold on to her senses. Her breathing quickened as his mouth pressed down and parted her lips, demanding possession. Her limbs went weak and she felt herself floating, whirling, and then came the sensation of falling. She wasn't aware of how she got there but she found herself lying on a soft bed of hay, her body intimately entwined with his, his strong thigh wrapped over hers and holding her tightly against him. All her senses were caught up in the passionate, demanding kiss, the ravaging, erotic play of his tongue demanding and receiving an immediate response. Her hands slid down his back and then worked inside his shirt and over his bare rib cage to revel in the excited heat of his masculine flesh.

His uneven breath fanned her skin as his lips and tongue made a trail down the curve of her neck. "I lied to you," he mumbled. "I did tell Bonnie to call you." The need she was fighting burst out anew, as his hand slid beneath the waistband of her blouse and caused a blaze to sweep through her body. With a gentle, teasing hand he sought first one breast and then the other, turning her flesh hot and damp. His mouth savored the taste of her, suffusing her with waves of sensation. And then his lips slid from hers, and she trembled with pleasure as he lowered his head. Dayna knew all was lost. She felt the intense desire she aroused in his strong body, the hard rise of passion heating her when he shifted and placed one leg between her own. Dayna tightened her arms around his back but his head lifted suddenly, startled, as a sound pierced the haze of sensations and emotions and froze the passion boiling her blood. The barn door closed with a bang that made her jump. A male voice called out, "Hey, Boss, I got . . . Ooops!"

Dayna tensed, frantically trying to push Brand away, but he stubbornly remained close. To her relief, the ranch hand at the door was so embarrassed by his intrusion that, after giving them no more than a cursory glance, he looked away. "S-sorry," he stammered.

Brand moaned so softly only Dayna heard. The hay rustled beneath her as he reluctantly slipped his arm out from under her. Shielding her with his back, he called the man by name, his irritated tone indicating the frustration he was feeling. "What do you want, Joe?"

Carefully keeping herself hidden behind Brand's broad shoulders, Dayna sat up, trying to make some order of her clothes while Brand received a strained apology. "I'm really sorry, Boss. I thought you were alone."

The hardness that had been in Brand's voice was gone, replaced by a controlled, commanding tone as he took one more deep breath. "It's all right. What did you want?"

"I got those two horses loaded in the trailer. I'm going to drive them over to Chino Valley now."

Brand rubbed the back of his hand across his brow, the sheen of his bronzed flesh indicating the aroused state he had reached. He nodded. "Fine, but come see me right away when you get back."

The wrangler tipped his hat toward the green eyes peeking out over one of Brand's shoulders. Dayna shifted, settling next to Brand, and as she came into fuller view, she received the ranch hand's admiring smile. With private amusement, Dayna watched the quick results of the withering glare Brand leveled at him. Nearly tripping over his own feet in his haste to get away from Brand's dark scowl, the man turned and made a swift retreat.

Dayna frowned as the door closed behind him. "Will he mention what he saw?"

Distractedly, Brand answered, "What did he see?"

"I don't know," Dayna replied, looking down to make sure her blouse was buttoned. "That's what's worrying me."

She pulled hay from her hair and Brand smiled,

lending a helpful hand and straightening her blouse. "He didn't see anything," he assured. "But he wouldn't say anything even if he had. Does it bother you that much to have your name linked with mine?"

"That is why I was looking for you," she reminded him. "I wanted to stop it." She looked away with frustration. "And now you've just made it worse."

"*I've* just made it worse?" he queried in a tone mixed with irritation and amusement.

Dayna threw him a look. "From what I've learned so far, it seems the ranch hands have been doing enough talking already. And I think you're responsible," she blurted out. "*That* is why I was looking for you in the first place. To tell you I want it to stop." Stronger words of reproach were on her tongue, but she remembered something else and grimaced. "Oh! I completely forgot. W.R. wants to see you. Tom's here and . . ."

"I know," Brand interjected.

"You do?" Dayna replied as he rose to his feet and began buttoning his shirt.

"Bonnie told me before you came. Once you came in I forgot. It's not too hard to guess why, is it?"

She could feel his gaze on her as she looked down at her clothing to see if she presented a respectable appearance. She knew he was waiting for some response. Standing up, she brushed the hay off the back of her jeans. "You're very single-minded."

"And you weren't?" he asked with a grin. "You were as intent on making love as I was."

"No, I was not," she denied, grabbing a few quick breaths. "You're just too experienced." An unreadable expression she had never seen before flickered in his blue eyes before he looked down and tucked his shirt back into his jeans.

"W.R. seemed angry. So I'd hurry if I were you."

He took a step toward her. Their eyes met and all the inner emotion that had been present since the first time she had looked into that blue gaze was there again. "Have you any idea what you do to me?" he demanded.

She knew what he did to her. She acted illogically when he was around. She doubted they were thinking about the same thing. "I know," she teased. "Love at first sight."

He sighed heavily. "You're such a cynic." Dayna opened her mouth to say more but his hands covered the sides of her face and his mouth descended on hers. Slowly insistent, his lips played with demanding gentleness, coaxing and persuasive. He stared down at her with a fierce hunger that numbed her senses, and then abruptly he released her.

A rosy hue suffused her face as his gaze reminded her of the closeness they had just shared. If he had drawn her back into his arms, she would have melted against him. But he didn't. He headed for the door and Dayna puzzled over how easily he switched off emotions as she joined him.

As they walked up the hill Dayna saw the looks exchanged among the ranch hands they passed. Brand might have been unconcerned about the attention they were receiving, but Dayna was thoroughly disconcerted by it. Unwittingly she was causing the very gossip she had sought to prevent. There seemed only one solution and that was to stay away from Brand. If she didn't, she'd end up being involved in a whirlwind romance that could do her more harm than good. There was something else she needed to remember—Alexandria Minter.

Brand frowned at the worried lines he saw. What was she thinking now? he wondered. She was the most stubborn, strong-willed woman he had ever met. He smiled to himself at the thought, for it was those very traits which annoyed him that also attracted him to her.

Attempting to lighten the mood between them, he regaled her with what he called "frontier wisdom" about one of the guests' unsuccessful attempt at riding a horse. Dayna smiled in response to the humorous account. There was something special about him and she knew now more than ever she had to stay clear of him.

Her frown deepened and he said, "A penny for your thoughts."

Caught by surprise, Dayna sought a safe topic to satisfy his curiosity. "Why do the ranch hands call you 'boss'?"

"Why not? That's what I am. I am foreman, or did you forget?"

Dayna laughed lightly but she was still perplexed. As Brand opened the lodge door for her, she commented, "I would think they would use that term for W.R."

Following her inside, he shook his head. "They never have. He's always been W.R. to everybody."

"What do they call Tom?" she asked, watching

him carefully to see if he disliked his employer's son.

A smile hovered at the corners of Brand's mouth, but he said, in a serious, deadpan manner, "Tom."

Dayna threw him a look of exasperation, and laughingly rebuked him. "You're impossible."

He smiled with amusement, glancing toward W.R.'s office. Talking on the phone, a stern-faced W.R. stared back. Tom, more relaxed than his father, sat with one foot propped on a nearby chair. Brand nodded to both of them. "I'd better go." His eyes caressed her face, warming her inside all over again. She needed protection. Not just from him but herself.

"Before you go, Brand, I want you to know that what happened in the barn won't happen again. In fact, it's all your fault it ever happened."

"I'll take the credit." He laughed softly but his smile faded at Dayna's sharp retort.

"I mean it, Brand," she said a little too loudly. Sara looked up from behind the counter, and Dayna repeated in a whisper, "I mean it. You make sure my name isn't linked with yours. I don't want people believing we're having some—some . . ."

"Love affair," he finished softly. "Seems to me you should have thought of that sooner," he mocked, the twinkling glints in his blue gaze reminding her of what had transpired between them in the barn. "Now, why don't you face the truth? You weren't fighting me. I told you, Dayna, we're destined to meet." A slow, lazy smile formed again, conveying that what he meant was much more intimate than the simple, spoken implied words.

Dayna released a shaky breath as Brand entered W.R.'s office. Inside, he greeted Tom Reardon warmly as an old friend. The exchange answered Dayna's question about the friendliness of their relationship. She watched until Brand slouched down in the chair across from the desk and next to Tom's, and then she started for her room.

As she reached the top of the stairs, she realized she wasn't sure what she was feeling, but of one thing she was certain. Brand Renfrow could only mean trouble for her. He wasn't much different from any other man, just more persistent. She had to remain indifferent to him.

Chapter Seven

$\mathcal{A}$ shiver swept through Dayna, but the predawn chill was well worth the sight before her as she sat on the horse and watched the absolutely spectacular sunrise. It was overwhelming. Streaks of light appeared above the mountains, turning the sky above the ragged cliff tops rose and gold. A gentle breeze swept her hair forward as she looked over her shoulder toward the chuckwagon that had accompanied them on the trail ride. A handful of wranglers, through their quick work and expert skill, managed to set before them a breakfast of flapjacks and sausages by the time the sun was warming the land. Sipping the hot coffee in her cup, Dayna realized that in just days her attitude toward the vast rugged land and the people who lived there had completely changed. That rough breed of men no longer seemed alien to her. She appreciated their honesty, which was rare in more metropolitan surroundings, and their casual, easy-going manners and friendliness complemented their genuine hospitality.

Conversation was lively and informative while they ate, the ranch hands sharing some of the land's history with the guests, relating the story of a five-year war during the 1880s between a sheepherder and a cattleman that resulted in the death of nineteen men and a period of vigilantism that sparked one lynching not far from where they were sitting.

When they returned to the lodge, Dayna anticipated doing nothing the rest of the afternoon but lazing around the pool.

The sight of the sheriff's car outside the lodge piqued her curiosity and she decided to go out to the front entrance and investigate.

She could have kicked herself the minute she opened the door and came face to face with Brand. He was leaning casually against one of the porch uprights, his arms folded across his chest, and he saw her immediately.

Deep in discussion with the sheriff, W.R. was a little slower in noticing her. "We don't know who's doing it, but it's becoming pretty obvious now with so many head lost that it's not an accident," W.R. said with a note of impatience.

"You aren't the only ranch to be hit," the sheriff assured. "Sounds like a rustling operation."

Dayna was nearly at the edge of the building when the sheriff made his reply. She frowned, wondering if she had heard him correctly, but continued on to the pool area.

She chose a shady spot under one of the lawn umbrellas placed around the pool, but within minutes she began to feel the wilting effect of a sizzling midmorning sun. The temperature was much hotter than she'd anticipated for this time of the year. According to the newspaper, a cooling trend was supposed to arrive in a few days, but that didn't give much comfort now.

With a large glass of ice water in mind, she rose from the chair and walked back toward the lodge. A searing heat of a different sort bore into her back. She sensed Brand's presence even before she whirled around. Lazily, he leaned against a palm tree with his arms folded across his chest, offering a smile that Dayna resolved to ignore. "Have you been standing there long?"

"Not as long as you've been baking in the sun." His features softened as his gaze slowly traveled along the glistening flesh of her shapely legs in her white cotton shorts. The sun was cool in comparison with his smoldering look as his eyes came to rest on the beads of perspiration that had formed in the deep V-neckline of her halter top.

"I have to drive around the ranch," he offered. "I could include a little sightseeing tour if you'd keep me company."

"No, thank you," Dayna answered, turning away.

"You're really not very polite sometimes," he drawled in an easy manner.

"Yes, I am," she countered, truly offended. As a travel agent it was imperative she display a friendly, polite manner and she couldn't ever remember anyone accusing her of being anything but amiable.

"Maybe I used the wrong word." His blue eyes narrowed speculatively, making Dayna feel as if she was being dissected and examined with every step he took toward her. Inches from her, he stopped, a taunting grin hovering at the corners of his mouth. "Maybe 'friendly' would have been more accurate."

"I *am* friendly," Dayna insisted.

"Not to me," he protested, lightly.

"I don't think you know what the word 'friendly' means. You confuse it with a much more sensual emotion."

"Where you're concerned the two feelings go hand in hand. But if you come with me, I promise to follow your definition of 'friendly.'"

Dayna tilted her head skeptically at him, not really believing someone as tenacious as he would keep his word about making no advances.

Drawing his breath in deeply, Brand wiped a hand across his mouth and, raising his right hand, he swore with mock seriousness, "I promise today to behave myself. Boy scout's honor."

"That's supposed to be reassuring?" Dayna queried. "I doubt very much you were ever a boy scout."

"I was a volunteer helper with the forest rangers when I was sixteen," he said lightly. "Would that count?"

"Nothing really would convince me," Dayna answered.

One side of his mouth lifted in a lopsided grin. His voice was confident. "But you'll go with me."

"Yes," Dayna sighed heavily, wondering why it was so difficult to say no. "Yes, I'll go," she confirmed, convincing herself he might just say something about Alexandria Minter. The idea of poking around and asking questions of other people about the matter really didn't appeal to her. If he said something incriminating she could go appeal to W.R. with the information. That would be much simpler. She nearly laughed in self-derision as she looked up and met the warm and sparkling blue eyes staring down at her. Nothing where Brand Renfrow was concerned was simple.

"I'll be back down in five minutes."

"I'll be waiting," Brand answered as she started to walk away. "For as long as it takes," he added softly.

She doubted he had meant her to hear his last words, but she had. An anxious shiver stirred by anticipation ran up her spine. As she changed her clothes, she asked herself really why she was going. She paused in the act of yanking on her boots, as the simple answer entered her mind. Until this moment she could pretend differently, but now, alone with herself, she was forced to face the real reason. She wanted to be with him. She shook her head in disgust and wondered how she was going to remain indifferent to Brand while she tried to find out about him and Mrs. Minter when much deeper feelings kept surfacing.

With an even more determined lift of her chin, she descended the stairs to the lobby, reminding herself with every step she took that she had a job to do. And, more important, she had to keep in mind that no matter what he said, he wasn't any different from all the other men she had met.

Surprisingly, Brand was true to his words. Not a meaningful look or touch passed between them while he pointed out different historic and scenic points of interest. And throughout the whole time, he kept asking Dayna about herself. Leaning back against the truck door, she giggled over his last question.

"What's so funny? All I did was ask you what your favorite flavor of ice cream is."

"What's so funny?" Dayna echoed laughingly. "You already bought me an ice cream soda and you didn't bother then to ask if it pleased me. You just made the decision we would have chocolate sodas."

He laughed sheepishly and shrugged. "It's my favorite." His smile faded. "I'd like to please you," he said seriously, "but you haven't been really cooperative. If I had asked first, we wouldn't have even made it across the street to the ice cream parlor. I hear the word 'no' coming at me more than 'yes,' so I just don't give you the chance to say it. Today is a perfect example," he mused. "Look what I had to promise in order to get you to come with me."

"Such a hardship," Dayna teased impishly.

He glanced briefly at her again. "Not kissing you is very difficult. Even more disconcerting is your stubbornness."

"Look who's calling the kettle black. You're the king of stubborn."

"Sounds to me like we'd make a fine pair, then."

Dayna looked out of the window as he brought the truck to a stop. Seeing Brand come around the front of it for her, Dayna opened the door quickly and joined him.

"This area," he said, gesturing toward the entrance shaft of an abandoned gold mine, "used to be one of the state's leading gold producers. An awful lot of people still think there's some in there," he added.

"I gather you're not one of them," Dayna replied.

"No, there might be. But I don't need those kind of riches. There are other things in this world to be more treasured."

He looked meaningfully at her, and Dayna quickly turned her gaze away. Spending too much time with him might be a mistake. It would be better for her if she never let herself become involved with him. She should have handled everything with greater objectivity. But that wasn't possible now. She'd known that all along. It was her own weakness for him that she had been struggling against all along. The most important question in her mind now wasn't whether Palmer Travel Agency's reputation was at stake because of Brand's romantic tendencies, but whether her emotions were going to get in the way.

As she stood near him, she viewed the remains of what had once been a working mine but was now boarded up. Raising her head, she lifted a hand quickly to shade her eyes from the glaring sun. The countryside was peaceful and serene; the quiet was soothing. The only sound she heard was the snapping of a twig Brand was distractedly breaking apart between his thumb and forefinger.

His gaze exerted a power that drew her to him like a magnet. He looked troubled as he leaned back against the truck.

"I think we'd better go back now," she suggested. She didn't expect him to agree with her request, but to her surprise he turned and moved toward the truck. She started to follow but paused in midstride as he lifted out a picnic basket from the back of the truck.

Tucking a blanket under one arm, he explained, nonchalantly, "I thought you might be as hungry as I am."

Dayna couldn't miss the double meaning of his word. Against her better judgment, she found herself reaching for the blanket. She spread it out under a nearby tree, even while she questioned her own actions. Why didn't she just refuse and insist on going back to the ranch? "What did you bring to eat?" she asked as she sat down on the blanket with a resigned sigh over her own submissiveness.

Brand joined her, placing the basket between them. "Pot luck."

Dayna laughed softly as she lifted the red-and-white checkered cloth and saw chicken legs, cheese, biscuits, two goblets, and a carefully wrapped bottle of wine. Her green eyes sparkled with humor. "You didn't know what was packed?" she chided lightly. "Who put the wine in there?"

"An incurable romantic," Brand answered seriously. Her hands became still. No more words were needed. She felt the color rising in her cheeks as she watched his eyes move leisurely and appreciatively down her body. She remembered the warm, firm touch of his lips and the granite hardness of his body when he kissed her. "I hope the wine pleases you."

Dayna knew his words were carefully chosen to recall their conversation just minutes ago, when he spoke of pleasing her if she'd just be more cooperative. A minute passed before she could speak in a voice that didn't quiver with anticipation. "It does," she answered, picking up the bottle and examining the label.

The meal passed pleasantly as they discussed their college experiences and first jobs after graduation. Packing the leftovers in the basket, Dayna watched from behind lowered lids as he lay down on the ground. His hat slid forward, hiding a good portion of his face, and he cradled one arm behind his head while the other hand balanced a glass of wine on his chest. Resting her chin and arms on bent knees, Dayna wondered if he was asleep or if there was another reason for his unusual silence. With some hesitation, she ventured a guess at what he might be contemplating. "I overheard W.R. talking to the sheriff. Was there another reason besides the desire for my company that made you invite me on this sightseeing tour?"

Propping himself on one elbow, he shoved his hat back. "Desire is an appropriate word. It seems to be controlling my every thought lately."

"I don't think that's why you've been looking so worried this afternoon."

Brand grimaced. "I didn't know it was that obvious. We've had a few problems lately," he explained. "The fencing is being deliberately cut. I thought maybe when we were driving around I'd see something."

Dayna hunched forward over her bent knees. "I overheard the sheriff mention rustling. Do you really believe someone is stealing cattle?"

Brand made another face. "Looks that way."

"Cattle rustling?" Dayna murmured with amazement. "I thought that kind of thing disappeared with the turn of the century."

Brand laughed. "City slicker. No, it's still around, though it's not quite as easy as it used to be."

His eyes locked with hers and Dayna tensed slightly. "You can ease my worries. Take my mind off them," he said coaxingly. Dayna started to shake her head. "One kiss," he said so softly it was a whisper, and he leaned toward her. "Just one kiss."

His lips brushed the side of her face and then roamed lightly and slowly over it, kissing her eyelids and her cheek and nibbling gently at her ear before his mouth barely touched hers. It was teasing and playful, his lips caressing first one corner of her mouth and then the other. Dayna's lashes fluttered and her eyes closed as the gentle kiss deepened and became more seductive, while his tongue tasted her lips. A rush of heat began to sweep through her even though his hands weren't even touching her, and Dayna understood the danger in just one kiss.

She pulled back quickly, drawing in her breath sharply, but Brand didn't move. His eyes looked puzzled. "You don't want me to stop."

There was too much truth to his words. Dayna clung to the only excuse she had as his blue eyes stared up at her, their warm softness as enticing and persuasive as his kiss.

"I don't let emotions rule me. I have a brain, a very good one. It tells me this is impossible."

His voice was husky and soft. "I don't understand. All I know is you linger in my mind. You haunt me when you're not around."

Wild sensations tempted her to forget everything —why she was there, Alexandria Minter, her father's concern for the reputation of the travel agency.

"Are you afraid?" Brand asked, seeking answers.

"I'm not afraid," Dayna insisted. "You're too fast."

"Don't banter with me now," Brand said abruptly, an edge of impatience creeping into his soft voice.

"All right. You're too experienced," Dayna answered, revealing one reason for her reluctance to relax with him and accept the emotions he stirred as genuine.

"I'm thirty-four years old, Dayna," he answered.

He heaved a heavy sigh; the edge of annoyance in his voice found an echo in his blue eyes. Rising to his feet, he offered his hand to help her up.

"I think we both want the same thing," Brand insisted.

Dayna couldn't respond—she wasn't sure what she felt at the moment. She drew a steadying breath as they walked back to the truck. They climbed in and Brand started the motor. His perceptive blue eyes were clouded with confusion. Dayna wondered if he could read her thoughts as he said bluntly, "You're looking at me with distrust. I don't know why. To be honest, I think I'm the one who should be on guard."

Dayna didn't understand why he was wary of her. She did know that he no longer seemed like the man she'd thought he was when they first met.

They were a half-mile down the road when, with a barely perceptible glance in the rear-view mirror, Brand unexpectedly swerved the truck to the right and off the road. Racing across the rough terrain, he brought the vehicle to a lurching halt that nearly threw Dayna against the dashboard. Only the iron strength of Brand's arm across the front of her prevented it. Without a word, he jumped from the cab of the truck. Dayna was shaken by the incident, and it took her a few moments to become aware of what was happening. She watched as Brand ran toward the fence and in one agile sweep jumped it and raced off after two figures.

Her heart was still pounding from the jolting stop, but as she caught sight of the two men he was chasing, even more frightening to her now was the danger he might be facing. Opening the truck door, she hurried after Brand, reaching the top of the hill in time to see him standing in the cloud of dust left behind by a white pickup truck that was roaring down the rough country road toward the mountains.

Brand whirled away, throwing his hat to the

ground in a gesture of disgust. "Damn!" he yelled before he looked up and saw Dayna on the other side of the barbed wire fence. Striding back toward her, he stopped and stared down white-lipped at the cut fence.

Dayna hesitated before asking, "Did you recognize them?"

"No," he growled and then squatted down. The muscle in his jaw twitched with suppressed wrath as he continued to glare at the fence with the look of a man who sees himself helpless. Dayna doubted that a man as used to being in control as Brand was could handle that particular feeling well.

He stepped over the fence, his hand lightly touching her arm. "Are you all right? I didn't hurt you, did I?" he asked.

Dayna offered a wan smile. "I'm fine."

"Do you want to wait in the truck while I fix this?"

"No, I'll wait here."

While he went back to the truck, she looked down the road toward the bottom of the hill. Clouds of dust, the aftermath of the truck carrying the culprits, were visible for miles. She glanced back at Brand and could tell by his hard-set features that he was blaming himself for not catching them. Whether it was logical thinking or not, she understood it. He was a proud man, the kind that didn't often get caught off guard.

Wearing work gloves, his head bent, he squatted down to splice the fence. She watched the concentration that turned his handsome features into rugged, hard lines. She was seeing him now in a totally new light. And what Alexandria Minter had said about him suddenly seemed not only impossible, but unimportant. Watching him work industriously at repairing the fence and seeing his anger at not catching the men, she realized just how important his job was to him—so important he was willing to tangle with criminals.

They were both quiet during the ride back to the ranch. In the silence, he reached out and caressed her face gently. As he left her at the lodge entrance, a rueful smile curved her lips. She watched him walk down the hill toward the working part of the ranch. With a deep sigh of confusion, Dayna returned to her room. She tried to call her father and made a face at the answering-machine message she received instead. Obviously he was out with Melissa, so there was no point in trying too long. Dayna wrote him a second letter, again saying that she hadn't discovered anything about the Minter affair but that she felt the need to write him. Her feelings for Brand were getting in the way of a job she had to do and the contact with her father, even if it was one-sided, helped to reinforce in her own mind why she was really there.

She knew there was only one solution to her problem—to find out what really had happened when Alexandria Minter was at the Double R. But every time she convinced herself to take action, she backed off.

Dressed in shorts and a T-shirt, Dayna felt just as reluctant the following morning to confront Brand or talk to W.R. about why she was really there. W.R. had enough on his mind at the moment with missing cattle. Some of the ranch personnel were edgier than usual. She didn't feel like adding to their woes at that particular time. Gathering a few soiled clothes, she went down to the back of the lodge where laundry facilities were available for guests. With a coffee cup in hand, she settled down in one of the blue director-styled chairs, and while the clothes were being washed she tried to concentrate on a book she had started reading in Hawaii. She thought she was succeeding, but the warmth of the sun streaking through the window beckoned her outside, making her realize how easily distracted she could be these days. As she stepped outside, she heard the sound of male voices becoming louder as they approached. She turned to go back inside.

"It's all set up." Dayna recognized Hank's voice as she touched the doorknob. "Now make sure you do your part."

Her brows knitted as the other man replied irritably, "I will."

"Don't get all in an uproar, Cutler," Hank said placatingly. "You tend to weasel out at the last minute. Just make sure you bring plenty of cash and do your part."

Dayna frowned over their strange conversation. She stepped back inside the building just as John Cutler passed by. Though she hadn't been introduced to the man, she recognized him as the ranch hand Christy seemed to devote her time to when Brand wasn't around.

Her frown deepened as she transferred her clothes from the washer to the dryer. Just what were the two of them talking about? With so many strange things happening on the ranch, she knew her wild imagination could probably come up with some ridiculous conclusions. She settled back in the chair again and picked up her book. What was happening really wasn't any of her business, was it?

When she returned to the room, Karen suggested a game of tennis and Dayna agreed quickly, glad for the diversion from her constant preoccupation with Brand.

After they had played one set, Karen suggested they go back to the lodge. Dayna couldn't blame Karen for not wanting to play any more. Dayna hadn't been much of a challenge. Her ability to concentrate on the game or anything else for that matter seemed to have deserted her.

As they walked away from the tennis court, Karen asked the obvious question. "Why aren't you with Brand? Is he working?" Karen tilted her head in a gesture of impatience at Dayna's refusal to answer. "Dayna, don't pretend with me. I've never seen you play such a lousy game of tennis. Now," she repeated, "is he working?"

"I suppose so," Dayna snapped. "How would I know? He doesn't account to me for every minute of his day."

"You only wish he did."

Dayna paused in midstride. "Karen, stop it!"

"Okay, okay," Karen conceded, "you don't care anything about him."

"I didn't say that."

"Dayna, stop fooling yourself."

"I'm not," she answered. "Love doesn't happen

this fast. Not that kind of love that two people should build marriage on. Very bluntly, he's told me he desires me."

"That's not news," Karen answered with a sly grin. "Anybody could have told you that. But be honest, have you ever dated a man who didn't?"

"There's an unbelievable tenacity in Brand." She couldn't help but laugh. "He's got so much determination that . . ."

"You're tempted to listen to your heart," Karen finished, making a face. "Would that be so bad?"

"Yes, it would. Casual flings can do a lot more damage than good, especially if one person in the relationship starts feeling a much deeper emotion than the other."

"Are you starting to feel something for him?"

"Yes," Dayna admitted, surprised at how easily the word came out.

"I know how cautious you've always been. And I realize someone who looks like you do has met more than her share of Casanovas, but maybe Brand is different."

Dayna shook her head. "He isn't. Are you forgetting what brought us here?"

"No, I haven't. But you don't know the truth yet."

"Maybe not, but I do know the difference between desire and love. You don't fall in love with a man in a week." Anxious to change the subject, she laughed mirthlessly and tugged at Karen's arm. "That's enough of all this serious talk. Come on, let's go inside the lodge and get a glass of iced tea."

At a loss for words, Karen decided to play along

with Dayna's feigned brightness, and she smiled and nodded in agreement.

Heads turned to admire the two slim figures, dressed in their revealing short white tennis outfits, but two men deep in conversation as they came out of the lodge were oblivious to them. Dayna was brought to a shocked standstill as she overheard one man's words.

"Hank, the boss has never been like this before. I asked him a question this morning," the wrangler rambled, "and I had to repeat it twice before he'd pay me any mind, and when he did he practically snapped my head off. He's as mean as a frustrated bull during rutting season. One of the guys who works with Charlie said the woman is from the city."

"Shut up!" Hank snapped. He shoved a hard elbow in the other man's ribs as he caught sight of Dayna and Karen standing by the door, watching and listening to them.

"What did you do that for?" the recipient of the jab asked.

"Dummy," Hank said in a loud whisper, glancing in embarrassment at Dayna, "that redhead's the woman. Don't look! Jeez! Are you stupid!" Hank scolded, grabbing the other man's elbow and hustling him away.

Karen had opened the door to the lodge but stopped and tilted her head wonderingly at Dayna. "What's going on?"

"If you're referring to their conversation, I told you," Dayna replied with a mixture of impatience and irritation, "he wants me."

"I've met my share of them," Karen answered. "But a woman doesn't bother them when she's not around." Karen raised a dubious brow at her. "I'll go order our iced tea." She closed the door behind her, leaving Dayna alone.

Dayna sat down on the porch swing. Swaying slightly, she turned her head at the sound of the door opening and smiled at Bonnie as he came out.

"What are you doing out here all alone?" he questioned.

She laughed lightly. "Would you believe meditating?"

"My daddy used to call that loafing."

Dayna nodded. "That's what I was doing."

She looked past Bonnie to the corral. Her eyes grew bright with interest as she watched a prancing white stallion circling with impatience inside the railed fencing. "He's a beautiful horse."

Bonnie glanced over his shoulder. "Proud bloodlines there. It shows, doesn't it?" he stated, his admiration apparent. "Valiant belongs to the boss. The horse isn't being ridden as much as he should be." His eyes swept over her outfit. "Been playing tennis, huh?"

Dayna laughed and flicked a finger at the tennis skirt. "What gave you that idea?"

Bonnie answered with a grin. "My keen powers of observation. It's part of good ranching."

Dayna laughed with him and then said more seriously, "It's part of being a good travel agent too. Maybe that's why W.R. and my father hit it off so well."

He nodded agreeably. "Could be. I've worked for W.R. a long time. He's a fine boss, real fair

with his people. And I'm not just saying that
because you're from the travel agency. Most people out here are real honest. You know how
Brand's always saying just what's on his mind.
Well, lots of folks here are like that. They don't try
to hogwash another man and take him for a fool."

Dayna nodded. She could personally vouch for
one man's bold candidness. Pain stirred inside her
at that faint reminder of Brand's offer and she
swiftly suppressed it with another question. "You
knew W.R.'s wife well, didn't you?"

"Sure did, ma'am. Beautiful lady. Real shame
she left us so soon. She was the kind of lady
everybody liked. Didn't matter who you were, she
made you feel welcome. Tell you, if it hadn't been
for the tykes he had, I don't think W.R. would
have wanted to keep going, but they needed raising. And let me tell you," he said, his eyes growing
bright with memories, "they were a handful to
bring up."

Dayna laughed. "All children are at times."

"You like little ones?"

At Dayna's affirmative answer, Bonnie replied,
"That's good. Real good. Some men just take
naturally to young 'uns. Brand does. He says if he
could find the right lady and she was agreeable,
he'd have six. He said there was sure plenty of
room to raise that many here." Dayna frowned
enigmatically. Bonnie shrugged his shoulders in
response, but his eyes were dancing. "Just thought
you might be interested in knowing."

"Is that so? Roscoe T. Bonner, I do believe
you're a romantic matchmaker at heart."

Bonnie guffawed. "Been called a lot of things,

little lady. Some of them not too nice, either, but never been called that."

Dayna smiled warmly. "I'm sure you've been called friend by many. But," she said, rising from the swing and turning to open the door, "I don't think you know what the Double R foreman really wants."

Swinging the racket in her hand, Dayna wandered through the dining room. Preparations were beginning for lunch, and fresh tablecloths were being laid down by Charlie's assistants. Dayna joined Karen in the guests' lounge and smiled at the sight of the tall, frosty glass of iced tea waiting for her. Slouching in a chair near Karen, she propped her feet on an ottoman and laid her head back, running the cool outer surface of the glass across her cheek.

Now that she'd seen Hank again, she recalled the puzzling conversation he had had with Cutler when she was doing her laundry.

"You're still wearing that troubled frown," Karen commented.

"I was thinking about something I saw today."

"What was it?"

Dayna shook her head and waved her hand in dismissal. "It's nothing important, I guess." She shrugged aside thoughts about Hank and John Cutler. They weren't her problem, but Brand was. And for even more personal reasons now Dayna needed to find out if Alexandria Minter's story was true. She had to know if he made a habit of seeking out female guests for a few weeks of fun and games.

Draining the iced tea, she set the glass down and rose to her feet. "I'll see you in the room, Karen. I've got a few things I have to do."

Dayna paused once she reached the lobby. She couldn't put it off any longer. She had to get some answers now before she allowed herself to become too involved with Brand.

Chapter Eight

*B*ecause of her association with the travel agency, Dayna had been given W.R.'s permission to inspect any part of the ranch. Dayna took advantage of that offer and wandered into the kitchen. Over another glass of iced tea, she was able to pump Charlie for some information. Despite her difficulty in following his broken English, she learned he had had his share of problems a few months ago, having to cater to the Epicurean whims of a very rich lady.

Dayna squeezed some lemon into her glass and asked matter-of-factly, "Was she here long?"

"No, missy. Only three days. Very angry when she left."

"She didn't enjoy her stay here?" Dayna asked, looking up. "Did something happen?"

Charlie looked over his shoulder at her, his

slanted eyes narrowing warily, and with a suddenness that didn't surprise Dayna, pretended he was
totally unable to comprehend her questions. She
didn't pursue the subject with him and sought out a
more talkative source. Bonnie was the one she
really meant to talk to, but it was Hank who ended
up being an encyclopedia of information. Dayna
eased him into the subject of Alexandria Minter. It
didn't take much effort, for she knew he was
flattered by her attention and would discuss anything. Offhandedly, she mentioned Charlie's woes.

Hank said informatively, "She was kind of high-
falutin. Everyone was supposed to jump for her. It
was as if she thought there weren't any other guests
here."

"Is that why she left so quickly?"

"No," Hank answered with a smirk. "I really
shouldn't say anything, but," he shrugged, "she got
more attention than she bargained for during one
horseback ride." He made a wry face. "We all
forget ourselves sometimes," he added, confirming
for Dayna that it was an employee Mrs. Minter had
been with. "She just left in a huff after that."

"If you have one bad apple you usually get rid of
it before it spoils the rest."

"Couldn't do that," Hank answered. "W.R.
wasn't here and . . ."

Wryly, she finished, "You can't run a ranch
without a foreman."

A heaviness settled on Dayna. In just days,
Brand had woven a maddening spell over her with
little effort. She had hoped the incident with Alexandria Minter wasn't true. She wanted to know for
sure if W.R. had been told but Hank, discerning he

might have said too much already, made a quick excuse to get away.

A frown settled on Dayna's face as she realized how much she had wanted to believe that Brand had genuine feelings for her. She forgot about Alexandria Minter while she was with him. She sighed knowing she had begun to believe his attentiveness and his flattering words. She raised her chin, angry with herself for caring about him.

After what Hank just said, she could only assume W.R. didn't know about the incident with Alexandria Minter. Out of loyalty to Brand, the people she had talked to who knew what had happened would have automatically taken a pledge of silence. But if W.R. did know, Palmer Travel Agency would have to exclude the Double R from their recommendations. Brand was another complication, a much more personal one. She could handle private emotions, couldn't she? Although there was a physical attraction, she was an adult, a mature woman, certainly not prone to infatuation that made one blind to the faults of another. But she had to admit to herself that she was much more vulnerable to Brand.

Head bent in thought, she wasn't prepared to encounter Brand at that moment. She entered the lobby, and her steps faltered as she looked up and was met by his piercing blue gaze.

He moved quickly toward her, grabbing her arm. "Come on. I want to talk to you."

Dayna balked, pulling back slightly. "What's the matter with you?"

"Come on. I've had enough of this."

"Enough of what?" Dayna flared in response.

His fingers tightened on her arm and he began to draw her along with him. Over Brand's shoulder, Dayna saw W.R. emerge from his office before she heard his softly spoken command.

"Brand, would you come here?"

"Could it wait a minute?" Brand asked tightly over his shoulder.

"No, it can't, Brand. I want to talk to you now."

Dayna waited, holding her breath, sensing the battle waging inside Brand.

"You and I are still going to have a talk," Brand said in a tightly controlled, calm, low voice before he turned and walked away.

Dayna hurried up the stairs, realizing that was the first time she had seen the temper that simmered beneath Brand's outwardly easygoing nature.

As she stepped into the shower to wash away the perspiration of the morning's tennis game, she heard Karen come in. Her heart was still doing a slow gallop when she finished the shower and slipped on her blue wrapper. Trying to ease away the excitement Brand's agitated state had caused, she decided to relax for half an hour until lunch was served.

Karen glanced up from the book she was reading as Dayna emerged from the bathroom. "Shelly left a note," she remarked, setting her book aside. "She and Martin are sitting in on a lecture by a visiting professor on archaeological sites of the Pueblo cliff dwellers of the eleventh century."

Dayna smiled over the lengthy explanation. "Do you think she would have gone to that without Martin?"

Their laughter was interrupted by a thundering knock on the door. Startled, both Dayna and Karen jumped. Dayna rose from the bed and approached the door. "Who is it?"

An angry masculine voice replied, "You know damn well who it is."

Dayna flung the door open, ready to meet Brand's anger head on. "What's the meaning of this?" she asked indignantly.

Brand's blue eyes blazed. "I'm going back downstairs, and fifteen minutes from now," he said with ominous softness, "you'd better be waiting at the stables for me."

His command took her by surprise. She found herself gaping at his retreating form and shut her mouth quickly.

Dayna closed the door and turned back toward Karen. What had provoked his ire? He certainly looked primed for an all-out war with her.

Stirred into action, she discarded her blue wrapper and replaced it with jeans, a blue cotton shirt, and her boots. Grabbing her western hat, she made a brief stop before the mirror and then hurried out.

Diamond, the bay horse she'd become accustomed to riding, was already saddled and waiting for her at the stable. Brand's eyes flicked over her breasts in the brightly colored blouse and down the length of her legs in the snugly fitting jeans. Dayna expected some remark, but without a word, they rode away from the ranch toward the grayish-gold desert. The only comment he made was to say that he had to ride out and check on some cattle.

He led the way at a leisurely gait, riding with the sureness of a man moving as one with the animal beneath him. For a long time, they rode along the barbed wire fence. She would have enjoyed the ride more if he had been a more cheerful companion, since she knew she was seeing the ranch as few other guests did. But the strong planes of his face appeared hard, and his mouth was tightly set in a determined line. She couldn't guess the reason for his foul mood. When he finally slowed his horse to a walk and rested one hand on his thigh and the other casually on the saddlehorn, Dayna relaxed, too, and made a stab at conversation. "Bonnie said the spread was big."

"There's a game refuge nearby. That way," he said, pointing to the west.

"I understand from Mrs. Whitaker there's supposed to be a couple of hundred species of birds around here."

"She's probably seen them all." He shrugged one shoulder. "If that's what excites her, who am I to question it?" His gaze slid to her, his voice suddenly husky. "You know what excites me."

Dayna looked away, ignoring his remark. "Did Mrs. Whitaker give you a demonstration yet on all the bird calls she knows?"

"Cut the small talk, Dayna," he exploded. "Silence is better than this pretense."

Dayna clamped her lips together, wishing now she had paid more attention to the direction they had taken so that she didn't have to depend on him to find her way safely back to the lodge.

The blazing sun was high in the sky, and perspiration had soaked through her blouse, molding it to her skin, by the time Brand was finished inspecting the fence and checking on the cattle. Blotting her face with her open palm, she let her eyes stray to him. His tanned face was wet, his shirt as sweat-marked as her own. She didn't want to complain, but she hoped he'd find some shade and stop for a few minutes.

As if reading her mind, Brand reined his horse to the right and led the way toward a small group of trees. He slid from the saddle and unhooked a canteen. Moving beside her bay, he offered her the water first. She gripped it in her hands and drank greedily, drawing a cautioning command from Brand. "Slow down. You'll make yourself sick."

As she handed the canteen to him, his hand brushed hers. Despite the time that had elapsed since they left the stables, anger still showed in his eyes. The quiet, brooding mood that possessed him was so alien, she couldn't help wishing for the return of the teasing, persistent man who bore an amused smile almost every time he looked at her.

Without a word, he grabbed the blanket from behind his saddle and walked toward the patch of grass under the trees. Dayna made a face at his back and squared her shoulders, bracing herself as she dismounted and followed.

Sitting on the blanket with his arms wrapped around his knees, he scrutinized her face closely, as if he could read some answers there. "I think it's time you were honest with me." As she sat on the blanket beside him, an anxious shiver ran up Dayna's spine. It took a great deal of restraint for her not to fidget beneath his penetrating blue gaze. "Out here you can't just up and run if you don't feel like answering. I understand you've been asking a lot of questions. Do you want to tell me what's going on?"

Dayna sat a little straighter, realized this moment was inevitable. "Yes," she answered. "You're right. It is time." Looking down, she plucked a few blades of grass and then tossed them quickly aside. "I am on vacation, but I'm also here to verify some information."

He shot her a look. "You're checking up on the Double R?"

"No. The ranch deserves its high rating. What brought me here was a phone call to the travel agency from one of our best clients about his wife's stay here. *You*," she said, meeting his narrowed blue eyes, "were the reason for the complaint."

"Me?" Brand asked, looking perplexed. He remained reclining casually but his fair brows knitted together.

"W.R. was in Dallas at the time. Since everything I've heard appears to be true, even if W.R. didn't know about it, it would be my responsibility to tell him. If he doesn't dismiss you, Palmer Travel Agency will have no choice but to discontinue our tours at the Double R."

His gaze rested on her. "Quite a businesslike lady when you have to be, aren't you?"

"We've spent a lot of years building a reputable firm. I'm not going to allow personal feelings to get in the way."

"So you've finally decided to admit there are personal feelings to get in the way." A corner of his mouth twitched slightly with a hint of a smile. With no trace of bitterness, Brand stated, "Alexandria Minter is the lady whose husband called."

Dayna nodded. "Yes. Your preferential treatment didn't find a receptive guest. Considering what I've learned, you're lucky she didn't press charges against you."

"That rich lady expected a great deal of special treatment," he answered meaningfully.

"Yes, but not the kind you were offering. And that's the point. You harm the Double R Ranch with that kind of behavior."

"There you go again. You've always believed the worst of me." Amusement danced in his eyes.

Dayna frowned and tilted her head questioningly, finding it incredible that he was taking the matter so lightly. "She was very specific. The foreman almost immediately started making advances toward her. You're good at that," Dayna commented wryly. "I know that from personal experience. I suppose I should say thank you for not forcing yourself on me as you did with her."

"I never felt the need to force you. Sooner or later I knew we'd reach a mutual agreement."

Dayna's green eyes flashed at him and her delicate jaw tightened.

Brand raised a placating hand and said soothingly, "Easy. I'm just teasing you. John Cutler was acting as foreman when she was here. I suggested he fill in for me. It was a case of poor judgment on my part to choose him, but he was qualified to handle the working ranch. The problem was, he thought his temporary authority extended to the guests. He shouldn't have had any association with Mrs. Minter, but he smelled a little money and moved in on her."

"Why wasn't he fired?" Dayna asked softly.

"Dayna, up until then he'd been a good, dependable worker. Since he wouldn't ordinarily have another chance to associate with the guests, it didn't seem necessary to fire him. It was my mistake for suggesting him. By the way, W.R. called Mrs. Minter yesterday and extended an apology to her."

"While Mrs. Minter was at the ranch where were you?"

"I figured that question was next," he said with a hint of a smile, though he rubbed a hand across his brow. "Try and remain calm," he ordered softly. "I was in Texas with W.R., buying some cattle."

He looked at her expectantly, knowing her sharp mind would fill in what he wasn't saying. "And you met my father?" Dayna asked.

"Yes," he answered softly.

A flicker of surprise touched his eyes as Dayna asked calmly, "Would you like to explain?"

"Explain what?"

Dayna shook her head in impatience. "You've been playing another little game with me. My father, too, it seems."

"Wait a minute. I don't know what your father has been saying. I'm sure he knew I wasn't the foreman Alexandria Minter was talking about. Apparently he was concerned and thought we didn't know about Cutler's actions. We didn't realize Mrs. Minter was that upset or that she'd complain to your father about Cutler. It was only after you told me you were going to visit the ranch that I got the idea that might be the reason."

"Yes, but when I suggested that Dad call W.R. he refused, saying he didn't want to offend his friend. . . . Don't you understand? He knew the foreman wasn't some long-employed, trusted friend and yet he led me to believe otherwise and insisted on sending me here to investigate."

Brand's eyes brightened with humor as he laughed heartily.

"What is so funny?"

"Looks to me like he was doing a little match-making."

"I agree," Dayna said, her voice lacking amusement. "But I don't think it's so funny. You knew who I was, you knew why I was coming here, and along with my father you've been having a great deal of fun at my expense, haven't you?"

"Hold it," he replied quickly, his smile slipping away as he raised a restraining hand. "I was being honest with you. Don't include me in that match-making scheme. I knew who you were because your father showed W.R. a picture of you. You looked familiar to me. I suppose that's why I first stared at you at the hotel and that's why I saw the exchange of money. I did misinterpret what I saw. After you put me in my place, I went down to the lobby and asked the name of the woman in room 101."

"Why didn't you tell me that you knew who I was, that you knew my father?"

"Do you think you could smile just a little?" One fair brow arched with resignation as Dayna refused to respond to his request. "Throughout dinner one evening in Dallas, your father spoke proudly about how competent and intelligent his daughter was. I guess after listening to him I knew as much about you as most men would after a couple of dates. I also knew that any man he liked, you obstinately shunned."

"I'm not incapable of finding my own male friends."

"I gather he thinks you should get married and is giving you a little push."

"You're not making points," Dayna said sarcastically.

"I know, but I'm being honest. He also told us how personable you were. I knew you'd be polite if you knew he and I had met. I didn't want that. I wanted to know those smiles were for me, not for some acquaintance of your father's. All I wanted was to be sure I'd have a fair chance."

Dayna restrained a smile, but his words touched her as she began to understand. "You almost didn't."

Brand smiled. "I know that it nearly backfired. I would have done better if I had told you I was in Dallas with your father and W.R. At least then you wouldn't have thought I was some lecher preying on rich married women." He smiled in self-derision. "When we began to suspect you might be here to find out what happened during Alexandria Minter's stay, I didn't understand why you didn't ask me right off about it." He laughed lightly. "Now I know why. All along you thought *I* was the one. Mrs. Minter didn't mention the foreman's name?"

"I really don't know. She may have. All my father said was that the foreman had made improper advances. What can I say?" she asked softly. "I really did have terrible thoughts about you. Would an apology . . . ?"

He leaned toward her, his hand cupping the side of her face. "A kiss would carry a lot more weight than words."

"It would?"

"Definitely," Brand assured softly.

He reached out his other hand, entwining his fingers in the mass of coppery tresses and drawing her closer while he pressed her down on the ground. Although he held his weight from her and his lips lightly, teasingly brushed over hers, the warmth of his body penetrated the paper-thin protection of their shirts. She touched his jaw with her fingertips while his lips played at the corners of hers as if to torment her for denying she ever wanted his kiss. She felt his impatience in the tense muscles of his shoulders as she slid her hands slowly around his back. She tightened her embrace, forcing him to offer the full pressure of his mouth. The kiss deepened, his lips twisting, becoming more possessive, his tongue probing and sliding over her teeth, tasting the sweet warmth of her mouth with a persuasiveness that took her breath away.

She was swept up by the heat of his body, and by the fire that had been kindling within her since their first kiss. She blazed with longing. But she knew it couldn't be because of love. Love didn't come that quickly. She couldn't yield and let desire rule her common sense. Though trembling with the passion he had aroused, she managed to break free.

Muttering, Brand sat up beside her. Dayna laid a trembling hand on her mouth and tried to breathe calmly. She glanced at him. The tight grimness of his lips declared the impatience that threatened to erupt. He drew a deep breath, his eyes resting on the front of her blouse. Instinctively, Dayna drew back when he reached out. When it became apparent he was only going to fasten a button she had missed, she sat quietly while he deftly manipulated the button with one hand. "You can't keep denying with words that you want me when your body and mouth just beg me to make love to you. Just be honest with yourself, Dayna."

Dayna waited for him to say something when they reached the stables, but he remained silent as he took both horses inside the barn. They were at the door of the lodge when he finally touched her arm in an affectionate, possessive gesture, something he had often done when they were walking. When they reached the stairway inside the lodge, Dayna nervously glanced toward the reception desk as the phone rang. She wasn't really sure Brand's anger and impatience had waned, and she faced him with some hesitation.

"Sweet witch," he growled in a low voice, conveying his exasperation by the use of her nickname. Then, the expression in his blue eyes softened and Dayna smiled in response. Desperately she wanted to trust him. "I don't . . ."

Her explanation was interrupted by the girl behind the lobby desk. With the phone tucked near her ear, she questioned, "Miss Palmer?"

Dayna nodded quickly and, as the girl extended the receiver toward her, Brand released her arm. "A long-distance call from Chicago," the woman said in explanation.

"Your father?" Brand asked.

Dayna responded teasingly, "My lover."

She moved toward the lobby desk and accepted the receiver from the desk clerk, glancing in Brand's direction as she did so. He stood at the end of the long registration desk, waiting and watching her, and she realized her lighthearted response may have been taken more seriously than she had intended.

Though a disturbed frown settled on her face she answered the phone with a breezy "Hello."

"Hello yourself," was her father's indulgent reply. "You'd think you were on the other side of the earth for all the communication we've had. Two letters, no phone calls. I thought maybe you ran off with some cowboy," he said, laughing at his own joke.

She could feel Brand's penetrating stare. It was ironic how close to the truth her father's words were.

"I'll be home in a few days," she said appeasingly to her father. "You know how it is when you're on vacation. The hardest thing to do is to write postcards. If you remember," she chided, "I didn't even get one from you when you took off with Melissa for Palm Springs." Not wanting him to belabor the subject, she asked, "How have you been? Is Melissa still on the scene?"

"I'm fine," Edward answered with a laugh. "And I think you may be going to a wedding soon."

"Oh, Dad, that's wonderful," she said, genuinely happy for him.

"I knew you'd be pleased," he said. "By the way, I assumed everything was all right there and you were taking a much-needed vacation."

Her father's next words were lost as Dayna's attention shifted to Brand. Without knocking on the door, he'd entered W.R.'s office. His back was to her, but even as her father talked, her mind could see only the outline of his features.

". . . know which flight you'll be taking and I'll pick up the three of you."

"Well, we haven't made arrangements yet."

"Honey? You sound preoccupied. Did I call at a bad time? Is there a problem at the ranch that would affect us?"

She heaved a sigh. There was definitely a problem at the ranch affecting her. Her anxiousness touched Edward. Since she became an adult, Dayna had proved to be strong willed, independent, and self-sufficient. Hearing an unaccustomed note of indecision in her voice, Edward Palmer couldn't disguise his concern. "Dayna, is something wrong?"

Was something wrong? Everything is wrong! Your daughter has allowed her heart and womanly instincts to get in the way of good common sense. "Nothing is wrong," she answered softly. "Dad, we were worrying needlessly. The man involved with Mrs. Minter was filling in for Brand . . ." She paused and then reprimanded him lightly. ". . . which I now understand you already know."

"I knew it wasn't him," Edward quickly explained. "My concern was they weren't aware of what happened."

"They were," Dayna assured him. "W.R. has called Mrs. Minter and apologized for what happened."

"Good," he said with relief.

Sure that if they talked too long, he might hear something in her voice that would lead to some embarrassing questions, she decided to cut the conversation short. "I have to go now. I'll call and let you know which flight we'll be on Sunday."

As Dayna handed the receiver back to the woman behind the desk, she tried to come to terms with her feelings. She moved on slow, unsteady legs to one of the sofas in the lobby and sat down. Except for Brand's brief moment of curiosity about her conversation, he was showing no concern or interest in what she did. He never pretended to be interested in anything about her but her body, she admitted honestly to herself. And in a way that was what was causing all her problems now. She, too, had felt the almost compelling attraction to him immediately. Call it what it is, she mentally berated herself—lust. But she felt a deeper emotion now, and it seemed self-destructive. What else could you call it when a woman began to have deep feelings for a man she'd known less than two weeks, a man who made it quite clear that his intentions had nothing to do with love?

Preoccupied with her thoughts, she was startled when Brand's voice whispered behind her, "Jealousy is a very dangerous emotion to stir up, Dayna."

"What makes you think it wasn't a lover?"

A mocking smile curled Brand's lips and he bent closer, his lips tenderly caressing the side of her neck. "Because," he said softly so no one else would hear, "I've held you in my arms and kissed you. There's no lover at home. But there will be one for you soon."

"Destined to happen?"

His eyes glinted with amusement, indicating that he had deliberately made the remark to arouse her. "I'll see you tonight. Meet you here." It wasn't a question. His voice carried the strong, assured quality of a man completely confident that he would get what he wanted.

Returning to her room, Dayna pondered whether she really wanted to resist the inevitable. Her thoughts betrayed her as she relived the feel of his muscular body, the pleasant, musky odor of his manliness, the warm, stirring, moist touch of his lips. Although she was so easily aroused by him, she didn't want to take part in a casual affair.

By dinnertime, she hadn't reached a decision, but she wanted to see Brand desperately, determined to be as candid with him as he had been with her. His absence at the meal worried her. Leaving the dining room, she decided to find him.

Luck was with her. As she stepped onto the porch, she saw Brand near the corral. He was leaning against a fence and holding his palm open with a morsel of food as a reward for the white stallion.

Dayna watched for a minute and then, ignoring the fact that her flimsy sandals were so ill-suited for the rough path to the corral, she hurried toward him. A hot evening breeze fluttered the soft material of her blue print cotton dress, but it couldn't cool her skin. The air was still hot and humid, and she felt it, clammy and warm, on the back of her neck and her bare shoulders.

As she approached Brand, the horse was first to react, lifting his head for a moment before turning his attention back to Brand's palm.

Leaning sideways next to him against the fence, she offered no greeting. Her smile said much more. "You weren't at dinner."

"I got busy," he answered, reaching into his shirt pocket and placing another treat in his palm in response to the nuzzling of the horse.

"I missed you," Dayna murmured. The words just slipped out.

"You did?" he asked with a frown. "That's nice to hear. You know there's only one cure for it, Dayna," he added, in a strangely emotionless voice.

She didn't answer. How could she deny what her body so obviously was shouting for?

"I told you we were on an inevitable course."

"I don't really believe that," she answered.

"You said you missed me. Didn't you mean it? Are you playing games, Dayna?"

"Aren't you?" she asked tightly. "You're the one who's looking for a brief affair, for casual intimacy."

An unexpected smile sent a rush of excitement through her as he said softly, "If we were really intimate the last thing we'd be is casual with each other. But you keep thinking that. I have to wonder if you've been fair with me. I could sit back quietly and never say anything, but," he said with soft irritation, "I'm not the kind of man who willingly allows himself to be led along." His eyes searched her face. "Why is it almost yes with you but always no? Have you been treating me to some form of teasing trickery?"

"No!" she answered.

"Then what is it?"

"Are you trying to intimidate me?" Dayna asked. "If you are, it isn't working."

"No, I'm not," Brand came back quickly, shaking his head. Even though his gaze held none of the tenderness and smiling warmth she had previously seen, his touch was as gentle as ever as his hand cupped her chin and forced her to look at him. "What is it that's holding you back?"

"Mature sensibility."

She could see the question form on his lips, but it was never spoken. Their eyes locked. "Then show me some. Be mature and show me some feeling." Dayna looked away in confusion. It wasn't stubbornness holding her back. Such an acknowledgment was a huge step, and she wasn't sure she could handle it emotionally. Loving a person seemed important. But how could she ignore the physical desire urging her to say yes?

Brand sighed heavily at her silence. "Okay, no more pressure—right now. But," he said with a husky laugh as he bent his head, "no more talk either."

His lips parted hers with an intimate kiss. It invaded not just her mouth but her soul with the depth of desire it summoned. It demanded a response—it insisted she yield to the emotions aching for release in both of them. She was breathless when the pressure from his mouth ceased. Quickly he released her, leaving her with nothing but an aching desire for more, and her lips throbbed from the brand of his kiss.

The corners of his mouth lifted slightly in the smile of a man who was aware from experience of his own persuasive power. Dayna tried to veil the excitement he'd aroused, but she realized she wasn't the only one to feel it—he was as breathless as she was. He was also more capable of hiding emotion. His voice was steady. "When you're through playing games, let me know."

"I've never played games."

"Yes, you have," Brand answered. "With yourself."

He turned away and began the long climb up the hill toward the big farmhouse. Absently Dayna stroked the stallion's nose. She wasn't playing games with herself. She knew exactly what she was doing. She had been protecting herself from making a mistake. But Brand's kiss was a powerful force. It was meant to make her feel she was being a fool for denying him. Deep down, she didn't want to stop him anymore. If she walked into the relationship with her eyes wide open, then she couldn't be made the fool, could she?

Impulse set her in motion after him. She would not have caught up with him, his long strides easily outpacing her attempt at running in her dress and flimsy sandals, but some inner sense made him stop in midstride and turn around.

As she reached him, slightly winded and suddenly dismayed about what to say, he flashed a smile, but questions mingled with the look of surprise in his eyes. "You flatter me. That's the first time I've ever literally had a woman chase after me."

Dayna couldn't respond to his jest. She looked at the patch of curly-haired chest that was revealed by the open collar of his shirt. He had stirred a deep longing inside her that logic could not make disappear.

She looked up, and his smile faded as his deep blue eyes, their gaze suddenly serious, called her to him. "Have we reached a time of truth?"

Womanly passions were roused inside her—she wanted to know him completely. Even though he might not feel the same sense of commitment as she did, she ached to be as one with him at least once.

His fingers caressed the curve of her neck with a soothing, circular motion, his voice suddenly husky with emotion. "Come home with me."

The touch of his hand stirred a pleasant kind of torment. The touch of his fingers moving slowly over her flesh and his passionate, hypnotic gaze conveyed the ecstasy she would know, the heights of passion to which they would soar.

A simple nod of her head, and Dayna knew there was no turning back. His arm curved around her waist as they walked down the hill toward his private room, which was attached to the bunkhouse.

Without hesitation, Dayna entered the room he called home, feeling closer to him just by being there. The knotty pine interior was totally masculine and much more pleasant than Dayna had expected. A large picture window looked out toward what was now just a dark outline of the mountains, but Dayna imagined that during the day it afforded a beautiful panoramic view of the terrain he loved. The bear rug on the floor and the elk's head over the mantle were obviously the trophies of a skilled hunter, an observation borne out by the bow and arrow standing propped up in one corner of the rustic room.

She smiled weakly, feeling excited, and Brand asked with surprise, "Are you nervous?"

"No," she admitted truthfully and moved forward to where he was standing at the foot of the bed. "I want to be here," Dayna assured him. "I want to be with you."

He took command of the situation. Leisurely, he caressed her throat, his fingers moving lightly down the slender curve of her neck. His hands touched her shoulders and her dress slid down as his hands skimmed the softness of her breasts, the slim line of her waist, and settled on the roundness of her hips. As her dress fell to the floor, an impish smile tugged her lips upward.

She pushed his hands gently away. "My turn," she whispered, opening his shirt and helping him slide out of it. A slight frown knitted her brows as she concentrated on undoing the buckle of his belt.

Dayna gazed at his bare body with an interest as great as he directed at her. There was something delightfully erotic about standing naked with him in the dimly lit room.

"My fantasies were dull in comparison with the real thing. You're more beautiful than I ever imagined," he said in a voice thick with emotion, his hands caressing her breasts, flooding her with tingling sensation.

"You, too," Dayna breathed, knowing that the

tenderness stirring within her spoke of much more than just desire.

She laid her hands lightly on his waist and stepped closer into his embrace, closing her eyes, her lips brushing the side of his neck as she experienced the first exciting moment of knowing the full length of his nakedness. The hair covering his chest made a soft cushion for her bare breasts, and the bold hardness of his body assured her of his virile strength. She trembled, aroused by the heat of him flowing into her, and she turned her head, lifting parted lips to him, slanting them across the firm, curving mouth.

His hand slid downward, pressing her against him. A moment later she lay beneath him on the bed, his granite-hard body pressed tightly against her, burning her flesh with their intimacy. His hands skimmed over her body with an indescribable thoroughness that swept liquid fire through her. Her hands were as curious as his, and her exploring touch felt the play of his muscles, first his shoulder and then his thigh, as she gently caressed the scar near his groin. He crushed her to him, his mouth covering hers again, moving over hers with devouring passion.

Their kisses became frantic, greedy, and reality whirled away from her, a heady mindlessness taking control as pleasure flooded through her. Every nerve in her body responded not only to the searing heat of his lips but also to the sense of power emanating from his hard body.

His body covered hers, his skin hot and damp from blazing desire, and she welcomed his body blending with hers in a consuming movement. She trembled as he came to her, gasping out her name. Her heart thudded fiercely as she responded to the primitive urgency of his powerful body.

Hearing his harsh breath in her ear, she knew he was as consumed by marvelous, wild sensations as she was. Closing her eyes, she pressed her head back into the pillow and gripped the hard muscles of his back, drawing him even closer, her slender limbs entwining with his as she arched her back in her effort to know total oneness with him.

Even later, she had no regrets. She reveled in the damp heat of his skin and the musky scent of their lovemaking. His harsh, disturbed breathing against her ear became less ragged, and his lips brushed the side of her neck.

Quiet, contented moments passed while she thought she would never want to move again. Then he shifted his weight from her and she nestled beside him. Her head rested in the crook of his arm, and his hands were gentler now, stroking and caressing the flesh he'd relished in the urgent heat of their lovemaking.

"I love you," he said in a husky whisper, kissing her temple.

Dayna swallowed hard as a giant lump rose in her throat. Why? Why did he have to spoil the moment? Why did he think he had to say those words? Why did a man as straightforward and candid as he was feel the need to lie now?

Dayna didn't answer. Within minutes, she could feel from the steady rise and fall of Brand's chest against her shoulder that he was asleep.

It took a Herculean effort to force herself to

leave him. She dressed quickly but glanced back once to look at Brand, one arm cradled behind his head, a sleepy smile of contentment slightly curving his mouth.

She closed the door of his room behind her and headed for the lodge. She would remember this evening as a special time they had shared and not allow the afterglow of his touch, which still warmed her body, to stir romantic notions that it could ever be anything more.

Chapter Nine

good morning." Karen's voice sang with cheerfulness and Dayna responded with a smile, unaware until that moment that Karen was even awake.

Slipping her legs out from under the sheet, Karen slid into her blue scuffs and headed for the bathroom. Dayna closed her eyes again. For a few minutes, she just lay there listening to the water running in the bathroom, her mind busy remembering the hungry desire of Brand's kisses and the deep needs he'd stirred within her. The need to feel his lips, warm and firm against hers, and to know the possession of his body was almost an addiction.

Slowly she raised herself and stretched to a sitting position. He said she lingered in his mind, she haunted him when she wasn't around. A soft smile curved her lips as she recalled the time with him last night. She felt content and peaceful. Being with him had been right; she knew, in the bright light of day, that the unquenchable passion they had shared last night wouldn't have remained unleashed for much longer. She felt light-spirited and filled with an impish devilment. She wished now that she had stayed with Brand and that it was his mischievous blue gaze she was staring up at, instead of Karen's questioning one.

"You look like the cat that swallowed the canary," Karen commented teasingly.

"You're silly," Dayna sighed, plumping a pillow behind her back and drawing her knees up to her chest.

Karen laughed softly. She didn't need to ask; it was obvious that Dayna was in her own private world that morning, one in which she saw everything through rose-colored glasses.

Rising from the bed, Dayna grabbed her robe and went into the bathroom to shower. As she stepped under the soothing spray of water, she knew how tempted she was to believe that a man could fall in love in such a short space of time. Although Brand had said the words, she forced herself to keep her feet on the ground. Those three little words were tossed around very easily by some men. A woman had to be cautious and exercise good common sense. She had to remember that some men sprinkled the words like powdered sugar on a dessert.

Minutes later, she emerged from the bathroom and, toweling her hair dry, she moved to the window to see the kind of weather that would greet her. It was another beautiful, cloudless day, destined to turn hot, judging from the bright sun radiating through the window.

There was a great deal of activity already, even though it was only eight in the morning. A truck was parked near the corral, and she saw Bonnie talking to the driver, whose two helpers began unloading the bleachers to be set up for the rodeo.

Some of the guests were returning from an early-morning ride along one of the ranch trails. Dressed in jeans and a red-and-white striped pullover, Christy was turning on the charm for John Cutler, her body seductively nestled close to his. Dayna made a wry face, surmising that Brand must not be anywhere near. The woman should be worn out from her efforts, she thought. Every time Dayna saw her she was batting those dark lashes at some man.

Dayna looked away as Christy exchanged a kiss with Cutler. But she frowned at the sight of two ranch hands gathered in conspiratorial conversation behind a maintenance shed. They were hidden, except from someone like herself who had an overhead view. Lingering, they repeatedly darted glances toward Cutler, who was slowly extricating himself from Christy's possessive grip. Dayna stepped back, not wanting to be noticed should one of them look up. The suspicions that had previously only briefly crossed her mind were intensified as Cutler joined the two men and handed each of them some money. She recalled the conversation between Hank and Cutler. Was it all some innocent exchange or were they involved in the cattle rustling?

She stepped away from the window and saw that

Karen had settled back on her bed again. It was hard to believe that Hank, whom Brand and Bonnie considered a trusted employee, would be involved in something illegal. She mentally shook her head to dispel the thought. But she couldn't, and even if it was nothing, she decided she should at least tell Brand what she had just seen.

At breakfast, the girls were joined by Martin and a Japanese industrialist who had decided to take a three-day side trip to see a western ranch. He provided interesting breakfast conversation, but Dayna's mind kept drifting. She had seen and heard too many things in the past few days, and at the moment she wanted someone else to know about them and lift the burden of the knowledge from her shoulders.

When Dayna questioned Bonnie about Brand, he merely shrugged. With W.R. also missing, the conversation began to lag. "W.R. eats with the visiting folks most of the time, but when Tom's in town they usually take their meals together in private." Bonnie rambled on, and Dayna sensed his talkativeness was the result of his discomfort over her own low spirits. He smiled, adding as an explanation, "When Joan—Mrs. Reardon—was alive, W.R. ran the cattle ranch and Joan just started the guest ranch. Shoat, Brand's dad, was foreman then, and the three of them worked hard to keep their heads above water. Joan did all the cooking and everything while Shoat and W.R. worked hard to build up the spread. In those days, they'd all eat here. But Joan made it a point that for special occasions—the holidays and birthdays for instance—they'd have dinner at the big house. She'd say that was a time for just family." He made a face and with a quick shake of his head added, "It sure was a shame she wasn't around long. Some beautiful lady, inside and out."

"Where was Brand's mother?"

"Never met her. Shoat came here when Brand was only two. I never really asked, but I guess the marriage just didn't work out and he took his son." Bonnie finished his coffee and shoved his chair back. Rising to his feet slowly, he said, "It's been real nice just sitting around talking, but I've got a few things I've got to do. Big day today," he announced with a smile. Keeping an eye on Dayna, he added, "Not too many more days and I'll be saying goodbye when I take you ladies to the airport. Guess you'll be kind of glad to get back to the big city, huh?"

Karen smiled in return. "Not really. It's cold back there."

Dayna took a sip of coffee but felt the need to say aloud just once what she was really feeling. "I'll miss being here. It's been like a second home, just as you said it would be."

Preying heavily on her mind was something she was trying hard not to think about—the necessity of leaving Brand. She rejected the thought and jumped up. With forced cheerfulness she said, "Come on, Karen, Shelly, let's see if we can find a fourth for tennis."

Bonnie moved away, shaking his head. He perceives more than he should, Dayna thought sadly. Mentally she fought the growing thoughts about love and shifted her attention to Shelly as Martin left them alone for a few minutes.

"Not me, Dayna," Shelly replied with a beaming smile. "Martin and I are going for a ride."

In mock astonishment, Karen said, "On a horse?"

"Well, yes," Shelly answered falteringly. "Why?"

Placing an affectionate hand on Shelly's shoulder, Karen grinned wickedly. "Do you vaguely remember you're the one who doesn't like horses?"

Shelly answered with a giggle. "Well, I do now."

"Uh huh," Karen replied with a teasing nod.

"Have fun, Shelly," Dayna offered. She turned to Karen, praying she wouldn't back out, too. "How about you? Tennis?"

"Sure," Karen said teasingly with a conspiratorial wink at Dayna. "Maybe we can each find someone like Shelly did and play doubles."

"Oh, stop it," Shelly beamed. "Quit teasing."

"Just so you know," Karen said, "we're both really pleased you've had such a good time here."

"That's right," Dayna agreed. "It's turned out to be pretty special for you."

Karen's smile disappeared as she mused that it had been special for Dayna too. But Dayna just wouldn't realize it.

At the tennis court Karen and Dayna found two recently arrived very eager partners. Introductions were made, and as one of them turned to join his friend on the other side of the court, Dayna rolled her eyes upward. "Our friend has fast hands.

Somehow he just couldn't turn away without brushing his hand against my leg."

"Oh, no," Karen groaned.

As they played the game, Dayna knew Karen was as grateful as she for the net that separated them from the pair of lechers on the other side of the court. As fast as politeness allowed, Dayna and Karen departed after the set, laughing and giggling over the pair they'd attracted.

For a brief time, Dayna had found a diversion. But as she walked toward the lodge with Karen, thoughts of Brand again intruded. She was filled with disappointment at not seeing him, and she wondered if she would always dream of him. When she was gone from the ranch, she reassured herself at first, she would forget him, forget what he looked like, just as she'd forget the other people she'd met. Sadly, she acknowledged that this was a lie. She'd never forget Brand.

As they neared the porch of the lodge Dayna's eyes turned a deep shade of jade at the sight of Brand near the porch with Christy.

Inching her body closer to him, Christy was inviting him to make a pass at her. Brand's face bore the amused expression Dayna had become so well acquainted with. He flirted easily, seeming to enjoy the opportunity.

Was that what he had been doing with her, too? Dayna wondered wryly as she stopped Karen from moving closer. The last thing she wanted was for Brand to see her or to get an inkling of the jealousy that threatened to erupt from within her. No strings, she reminded herself. She had gotten caught up in the rapture of his kisses, in the soft persuasiveness of his words, in the ecstasy of physically loving him.

It was Karen's voice softly repeating her name that made her realize she was clutching her friend's arm with a death grip.

As she looked up at Karen, she did her best to veil the turmoil of emotions coursing through her. Instinctively Karen queried, "Are you all right?"

"Fine. I'm fine." Dayna feigned a smile as Karen's eyes turned to Brand, who was now moving away from Christy.

Dayna urged Karen around the building to another entrance so they wouldn't be noticed, then left her in the gift shop and wandered toward the lobby.

A poster caught her eye. It announced a play she had missed seeing in Chicago. It was to be presented in Phoenix about the middle of the month. She shrugged her shoulder; the information was useless to her, since she wouldn't be in Arizona then. She sighed lightly, wondering how she had managed to avoid so many situations in her life and yet had stumbled into this one so unexpectedly. It gnawed at her that Brand was with Christy now. She wanted to be the one he spent every moment with. Last night she had convinced herself that she was walking into the relationship with Brand with her eyes wide open—that she would be able to walk away when it was over, remember the time she'd spent with him with fond memories, but that that would be the end of it. The heavy pressure she felt against her chest now made her wonder if all that was really possible.

She started to turn away but was startled by

Brand's unexpected appearance. He was standing
so close behind her that her shoulder brushed his
chest as she turned and she found herself in his
embrace, his arms surrounding and steadying her.

His eyes glinted with amusement. "Sorry. Scar-
ing you is the last thing I wanted to do."

Dayna shook her head. "You just surprised me."
Noticing he held a bundle of letters in his hand,
Dayna turned the conversation to them. "You have
the mail."

"One very sweet-smelling one for Hank from a
lady who lives in Yuma," he said laughing.

Dayna suddenly felt on edge. "I was hoping I'd
see you . . ."

"The feeling was mutual," he said softly as he
moved closer to her.

Inwardly Dayna tensed, finding his words difficult to believe, since she'd seen him with Christy.
She looked away, toward the window, fearful that
those blue eyes would see too much, would know
that a deep emotion was gnawing at her.

He appeared completely unaware of her emotional state. "I see you've been playing tennis." His
gaze floated lightly over her sun-browned legs,
revealed by the tennis outfit she was wearing.
"Have you met the Double R's answer to McEnroe
and Evert-Lloyd, just arrived yesterday morning?"
he asked lightly.

Dayna couldn't help laughing at his description
of the California couple, tennis club champions,
who had been boasting of their prowess since the
moment they had arrived at the ranch.

"He's been goading me," Brand said with
amusement. "Rodeo champions are not athletes,

so the gentleman says. I think you and I are going
to challenge them to a game of tennis."

Dayna made a face. "Can we beat them?"

"Sure we can." He touched a strand of hair near
the line of her jaw as if he couldn't resist it. "We're
a winning pair."

Dayna pulled back from his touch, determined
to shift the conversation to a less amorous topic
and tell him the puzzling scenes she had seen. "In
the last couple of days, I've . . ."

Dayna's words were cut short by W.R. "I've
been looking for you," he said to Brand as he
strode from his office toward them.

"I just got back a few minutes ago," Brand
explained, turning toward him.

"Well, what happened?" he queried with a hint
of impatience.

Brand heaved a sigh. "The cattle got out again
and were running. We went out in a dozen different
directions and got them rounded up. I took some
men and we rode back to look for drifters."

A frown etched deep lines in W.R.'s face. "You
think maybe coyotes spooked them?"

Brand threw him a meaningful look. "Did they
gnaw through the fencing, too?"

"I didn't know more fencing was cut."

"Well, it was. Even more puzzling, it was cut at a
point so far away from the road that the rustlers
would have had to drive across hundreds of acres of
our property before they'd be on the highway."

W.R. tilted his head to the side questioningly.
"What do you make of it?"

"I think they're trying to throw us off guard. The
cut was made and none of the cattle were taken. To

me it all seems like a diversionary tactic. Well, anyway, I've still got a few men out checking on the herd."

W.R. ran a hand across his forehead. "I talked with four other ranchers this morning. They're all missing cattle except old Zeke Marlow."

Brand made a face. "He wouldn't know if he was missing cattle or not. He hasn't checked on his herd in years, so what he does have are like wild deer."

"That's true. He doesn't keep track of his cattle, but that's because he hasn't got someone like you around to keep an eagle eye on everything."

"I don't seem to be doing such a great job right now," Brand muttered.

"You're doing all right," W.R. assured him.

"Well, remember one thing," Brand stated. "They might have the stolen cattle corralled somewhere, ready to transport. If the brands have already been altered, we'll have a hell of a time proving they're ours even if they are caught."

Standing silently beside Brand and listening to their conversation, Dayna hesitated, unsure if what she'd heard was even worth telling. She touched Brand's arm lightly, drawing both his and W.R.'s attention. "I heard something the other day, but I'm not sure it means anything." Dayna related quickly and simply the conversation she had heard between Hank and Cutler. Even before she had finished, Brand was smiling.

He shook his head. "It's nothing, Dayna."

"But what about the money? Don't their words seem strange to you?"

"They were talking about the poker game set for tonight."

"Hank told Cutler he'd better not back out," Dayna added. "That sounds a lot more sinister than some poker game." Feeling exasperated at not being able to convey the cloak-and-dagger tone of the conversation she'd overheard, Dayna stressed, "Hank sounded very serious. It didn't sound like they were discussing something as simple as a poker game."

Brand laughed softly. "Sweetheart, out here poker games are not simple." Dayna was warmed by his endearment and looked at W.R. self-consciously. The twinkle she saw in his eyes assured her that he, too, had noticed the affectionate term.

Unmindful of the look Dayna was exchanging with W.R., Brand added, "They've held about four poker games since Cutler started working here and he said he'd be there for every one of them and wasn't. I think the hands are getting a little annoyed because he's always shooting off his mouth about how good he is."

His explanation was logical but Dayna still felt uneasy, remembering what she had seen earlier that morning. "But I saw Cutler and . . ."

"Ssh." His finger touched her lips. "I appreciate your playing Mrs. Sherlock Holmes, Dayna, but I'd stake the best quarter horse on this ranch that Hank's innocent."

W.R. nodded in agreement. "He's been with us too long, Dayna."

"What about Cutler? This morning I saw him exchanging money with two other men."

"I told you," Brand said lightly. "With the poker game set for tonight, that's really not so strange.

And there are always a lot of parties going on after the Double R's annual rodeo. It's a big night with the ranch hands. Now don't worry about it anymore. Okay?" he urged.

Dayna shrugged in resignation. "Okay," she agreed.

W.R. massaged the back of his neck with his hand as if he needed to soothe knotted muscles. "Let's try and keep everything as low-keyed as possible concerning the problems we're having. We don't need any undercurrent of trouble with the rodeo going on today. I understand you drew Soft Touch."

Brand laughed. "Sure did."

"I was surprised when I heard you were competing."

"I've got a score to settle with that old bull."

"Hope he doesn't think the same thing," W.R. said wryly. With a parting nod to Dayna, he returned to his office.

Their conversation had been light and bantering, but Dayna felt just the opposite as she recalled how she had baited Brand that day, how she had practically called him a coward. "You aren't competing, are you?" Brand nodded.

"Why?" She couldn't keep the alarm from her voice as a feeling of guilt swept through her. "Is it because of what I said?"

Tenderly, he cupped the side of her face with his hand, his fingers burying themselves in her hair. "No, it's not because of what you said. I made the decision before you ever arrived."

"I didn't call you a coward."

Her anxiety could be heard in her voice and his

eyes narrowed slightly, searching her face for answers. "I have to do it to prove something to myself. Soft Touch is the damn bull that threw me. I have to ride him."

"You don't," Dayna countered.

"I do, Dayna."

His voice held a note of finality. Dayna looked away, pulling free from him. "You're so stubborn," she muttered. "Go on, then, and break your neck. I don't care."

Brand sighed in exasperation, but a moment later his hands were lightly stroking her hair as he forced her to look up at him. His voice was soothing. "Careful, sweetheart. For all your denials, you keep revealing concern—and jealousy," he added, making Dayna aware that he had seen her when he was with Christy earlier. "They're honest feelings that go hand in hand with a much deeper emotion."

Brand's words haunted her even after they separated—there was too much truth in them. Was she in love with him? That thought afforded her none of the joy and euphoria that everyone sang about. She shook her head, refusing to believe it. After all the years of caution and sensibility it was impossible that she had fallen in love with a man she hardly knew.

She returned to her room to shower and change. By the time she and Karen left the lodge, the grounds near the stables were filled with rows of pickup trucks and horse trailers. Country and western music blared from radios, the twanging sounds entertaining the stands of spectators sweating in the midmorning sun.

As she saw the competitors pinning number cards to their backs, Dayna sensed their feeling of showmanship. It was a matter of pride—and a serious business to them—to make a good showing before these hometown people, people who had probably known some of them since the day they were born.

Dayna and Karen overheard one wiry ranch hand, ambling ahead of them saying in a raspy voice, "Brand said to set it up in the barn for around eleven-thirty. Everyone should be settled down by then. Hank's to get the big coolers from Charlie before dinner so that the beer will be cold, and Cutler is supposed to pick up the beer some-time today."

"He'd better, if he knows what's good for him."

The man's comment went unanswered by his companion, who, totally preoccupied with joyful thoughts of his own imminent triumphs at the rodeo, said with determination, "I'm telling you I feel lucky." Rubbing his hands together with glee as if already victorious, he added, "I'm gonna take a good part of the winnings tonight."

The other man guffawed. "The only thing you ever take back to the bunkhouse is a sure-fire reason for a hangover the next day. Just remember, even if you can't walk a straight line tomorrow morning, you'd better pretend you can. The boss never gets drunk, so keep that in mind when the room starts spinning."

Dayna didn't listen further. Her attention shifted to Brand, who was standing with some of the other contestants behind the chute area. He was working something into the palm of his glove.

"What's he doing?" Karen asked Bonnie, who had just come up beside them.

"He's working rosin into the glove," Bonnie answered. "He'll tie leather straps around the top of his boots and his wrist later to make sure he doesn't lose the boots or the glove during the ride."

Dayna nodded in reply, trying to appear calm, but her stomach was somersaulting with anxiety. Bonnie's next words didn't ease her tension. "Brand holds the rope hard and tenses his whole body, using all his muscles to move with the bull. A smaller man can't do that. To be a good bull rider a man's got to have a strong arm, because those muscles keep the rope tight on the bull and himself seated."

"Isn't the rope secured to the bull in some way?" Karen questioned.

"The rider's grip is what holds it," Bonnie stated.

Dayna looked away, tugging Karen's arm so she'd start walking again; then Bonnie would have no chance to mention the danger she was sure Brand would be facing. The sight of one hulking bull being led to the chute area made her start to walk quickly away. Up until that very moment she hadn't allowed herself to consider how dangerous bull riding was. But standing close to the animal, she was startled by his enormous size. Visions of Brand being crushed or trampled or gored by the lethal-looking horns ran through her mind. With dismay, she became aware of what she had been trying desperately to deny. Love. She was in love with Brand. The thought disturbed her deeply, and she found herself caught up in a state of uncertainty as she and Karen inched their way through the crowd until they found seats in the stands.

The row in front of them held many familiar faces—the noncompeting ranch hands of the Double R had congregated there. Guzzling beer, they joked and wisecracked about the competitors, the fierceness or meekness of the animals, and the female spectators attending the rodeo.

Their attention shifted suddenly as if they were a unit. All eyes were fixed on Christy, who was sauntering along the front row looking for a seat. Dressed in brief yellow shorts and a scanty blue halter top, the leggy brunette paused and lingered, obviously trying to catch someone's attention. Dayna understood who it was she was looking for as she saw Brand and Bonnie climbing the bleachers toward them.

Hank, sitting in front of Karen, leaned to one side and made a whispered comment to the man next to him, drawing a whoop of laughter from him. Dayna caught the man's comment: "Bet we don't see our foreman at the poker game tonight."

Dayna gritted her teeth, her eyes hurling daggers at the back of the man's neck. If anyone was going to be with their foreman tonight, it would be herself, she thought with steely determination.

She felt even more confident of it as Brand winked at her before turning to sit down in the space the men in front of her had made for him.

Settling down on the bench next to Karen, Bonnie remarked to Brand, "Think we're going to see a couple of good old boys flattened today."

Brand's shoulders moved slightly with mirth, but

Hank looked over his shoulder at Bonnie and asked, "Did you see number 6?"

"Gentle Ride," Brand said.

"Jake Everett's youngest drew him."

"What a way to get initiated," one of the men commented with a shake of his head.

"That's nothing," Hank chuckled, looking meaningfully at Brand. "Hear you got another chance at that ornery bull. You're a glutton for punishment."

"He can be ridden," Brand answered smoothly.

"Oh, yeah," Hank agreed. "Twelve times in over three hundred tries."

Brand chuckled. "That's why he's called Soft Touch."

The men laughed at his comment, but Dayna shared none of their humor as Hank went on, "I suppose since you rode him successfully once you figure it can be done again. But he's the meanest darn bull I've ever seen even after the ride. That set of horns he's got must be nearly five feet wide."

Brand shrugged noncommittally and Dayna looked down, unconsciously wringing her hands. Inwardly, she felt as taut as a tightrope; Hank's words had only intensified her worry. She was tempted to lean forward and kiss the side of Brand's neck and beg him not to compete. She felt the possessiveness that is inevitable when someone else's body becomes as familiar as your own. He was her lover.

She concentrated on the announcer, who was greeted by applause and whooping shouts as the rodeo began. When the steer-roping event began,

Brand leaned back to answer one of Shelly's questions. His body was so close to Dayna's legs that the heat of his flesh penetrated her jeans.

Dayna became caught up in the activity of the rodeo as she watched the speed and agility of the horses in the woman's barrel-racing event. It wasn't until a lull in the action that she realized Brand was gone. All the stomach butterflies she had suppressed returned. She tried to concentrate on the event, but as every contestant was bucked by the high-spirited, wiry mounts, her thoughts returned to Brand. Wouldn't he shortly be pitting himself against a much more dangerous animal?

"He pulled leather," Hank commented with a snort of disgust, claiming Dayna's attention. She looked at Bonnie.

"The rider's disqualified," Bonnie explained. "Took hold of the saddle."

Dayna nodded as she watched the pickup man helping the rider off the bronc. But Karen's nudging elbow brought her attention to the chute area and the rambunctious bull it held.

"Just as dangerous for the rider inside the chute," Bonnie muttered more to himself than anyone else. As Dayna frowned at him, he explained, "Bulls do their darndest to jam or crush a rider against the side of the chute."

There was excitement all around her, but all she felt was tension. It was apparent by the enthusiastic applause that bull riding was the favorite event among the majority of spectators. But she questioned the sanity of the men competing. The prize money scarcely seemed worth the risks involved. She found the wisecracks of the cowboys seated nearby without humor as she watched each competitor receive a bouncing and jostling ride that should have broken every bone in his body. As each competitor scrambled to get away from the kicking bull, two of the clowns jumped in to divert the bull's attention and negotiate him back to a chute.

The young man on Gentle Ride successfully completed the required eight seconds, but when he jumped from the bull, the animal kept spinning, trying to butt him.

Dayna's heart was thudding even after the man was safely perched on top of the fence. "Why don't they use a pickup man?"

Hank looked back at her and answered, "In bronc riding the horse avoids the man after he's thrown off, but a bull doesn't. He'll go after anything he sees, even a horse. He doesn't care what he gets. He's just hell-bent on stomping or goring anything he can find."

She heard Brand's name announced, and for a split second, she imagined what could happen if he was thrown from the bull or if his leg was damaged again. Every instinct she possessed urged her to leave the stands as the bull slammed against the side of the chute. Brand stood poised above it, his weight not even on the animal yet. She couldn't leave; she felt paralyzed, frozen with trepidation.

"He's the rankest bull I've ever seen," Hank commented, but Dayna heard admiration in his voice.

Dayna drew a deep breath as Brand gave a signal and the gateman opened the chute. The bull charged forward and for eight bone-jarring seconds

Brand was caught in a maelstrom of bucking, stomping, twisting, and spinning while the crowd yelled encouraging words. The bull leaped off the ground, all four feet in the air, while he kicked and bucked trying to jerk his rider off. Brand hung on with determination, his whole body moving with the animal, despite its ferocious efforts to be free of him. Finally, the buzzer rang and Brand, waiting until the bull was in a high arch, vaulted to the ground.

Dayna gasped with alarm. The bull reversed its direction, his hooves coming down frighteningly close to Brand. She was shaking and breathless with heart-pounding fear.

Brand rolled away while two clowns hurried forward to distract the bull. Brand made a hair-breadth escape to the fence as one clown slapped his derby hat at the bull and then scurried to the fence and the other clown rolled a barrel toward the animal, offering him something harder than a man to ram his horns at.

"If he'd had clowns that good last time, Brand wouldn't have gotten gored," Bonnie stated with admiration.

Dayna released the breath she had been holding and smiled at him. "They *are* good," she said over the crowd's appreciative applause as they heard the high mark Brand had received.

Her shoulders slumped slightly. She felt as physically drained as if she had been with him on the bull. Her adrenaline was pumping fast as she turned to Bonnie. "Brand's good, isn't he? I mean really good."

With a hint of pride, Bonnie nodded. "He was on the professional circuit for a short time, but when his dad died he dropped out. He only enters local rodeos now, and not many of them since the accident. I knew the minute he heard Soft Touch was among the stock he would enter. He was hoping he'd draw him." Bonnie looked at her. He was aware of her anxiety and hoped she understood now. "A man has to prove things to himself sometimes."

"I guess so," Dayna answered weakly, comprehending now why Brand had competed, and realizing it was that same stubbornness that had provoked his tenacious pursuit of her. It was a part of him that annoyed her at times, but also elicited her admiration.

For the right woman, he could be the perfect man. She knew his gentleness, his sense of humor, and his skill as a lover. He was a man's man, yet he possessed the tenderness a woman sought. But as much as she wanted it to be so, she didn't believe she was the woman for Brand. Maybe, if they had more time together . . .

She caught the last of the announcer's words. People rose to leave, and her lips curved in a wide smile as she saw Brand working his way up to her. When he reached her, she raised herself on her toes and offered him a light, congratulatory kiss. His arm tightened slightly around her back, insisting on a more intense kiss before he allowed her to move away from him. A few of the ranch hands sent knowing looks in their direction, but Brand paid no attention to them and Dayna suddenly didn't care who saw the emotion between them. "How's it feel to be a winner?" she asked.

His eyes were caressing her again, and his hand touched her cheek before his fingertips slipped lightly across her lips. "I've been a winner since the day I met you."

Her breath quickened as his gaze burned into her. "Are you free today? Or do you have work to do?" she asked.

Appearing pleased by her question, he smiled. "No, I'm not and I do. I'm cooking tonight."

Dayna smiled at his self-deprecating grin. She would have continued the banter but became intensely annoyed when she noticed Christy impatiently waiting for Brand to come down to the lower stands.

Brand looked briefly over his shoulder in Christy's direction. A sardonic smile lifted the edges of his mouth as he looked back at Dayna. "My preferential treatment is limited to only one special woman."

"For the moment," Dayna said dryly, drawing an amused laugh from Brand before he left.

Dayna scanned the dinner crowd. Picnic benches had been brought out for the event, and a makeshift stage had been set up in front of a haystack. Campfires were ablaze around an old-time chuckwagon, and the air was filled with the enticing aroma of the dinner being prepared by the ranch hands who were standing over a variety of black kettles.

As she sat down next to Karen, Dayna saw

Brand hunkered down beside an enormous cast-iron kettle hanging on a tripod of sticks over a fire. Her eyes danced with enjoyment at the sight of such a strong, virile man, a man whose life and occupation were so decisively male, stirring the steaming contents of the pot.

People wandered around, conversing with the wranglers and waiting with anticipation for the sound of the large dinner bell.

It seemed that before dinner could start, some ground rules had to be observed. Dayna listened in amusement as W.R. stood before the microphone on the makeshift stage and spoke.

After greeting all the guests and making them welcome, he explained, "Now, just as they would do at an old-fashioned wrangler dinner, you've got to do your part, too, before you get the grub. Everyone get into a single line, starting where Hank is standing over there," he said, pointing a finger at Hank. "Get your tin plate and cup from him and then keep moving—first to the man with the most mouth-watering barbecued beef you've ever tasted, then on to the potatoes, the corn, the beans, the biscuits, and finally to yours truly for your peach." He smiled broadly. "Now there's to be no dilly-dallying. Just like in the old days, every man serving has his job and a special place on your plate to put the food he's serving. This is serious business, you know," he said with a feigned frown. "When those wranglers came in from being out all day on the range, they were mean critters—hungry and tired—and they wanted their vittles fast. Okay then, if everybody's ready—here goes." With a nod of his head to Charlie, the dinner bell was rung.

The novice diners held back a little, watching as those familiar with the workings of the serving line went ahead. Just as W.R. had said, they were each handed a tin plate and cup and began moving along the line. Dayna overheard an elderly man behind her remark, "The efficiency here could put an army mess hall to shame."

With remarkable speed the food was placed on each plate. As Dayna drew near Brand, she tilted her head to watch the serious expression on Brand's face as he carried out his job. When she stood before him, tin plate thrust forward to receive her share, he ladled beans on her plate, but a wink and a smile were added to her portion before she moved on.

The man of the hour was W.R., biting his tongue and wrinkling his brow with intense concentration as he gently maneuvered a peach half onto each of the plates in the designated area between the biscuits and the ear of corn.

After the meal, a country and western trio lent their twanging voices to various old and new western songs while in the distant hills coyotes howled their own nightly song. It was an evening Dayna would long remember as the guests were treated to what she considered the highlight of the evening— heartwarming performances by the ranch personnel: singing, guitar playing, a spoon-playing song by one of Charlie's assistant cooks, and other amateur talents.

All night Dayna had been watching Brand and

had seen his eyes fixed on her. She tried to keep her attention on the entertainment, but she was all too conscious of him. With a pretense at gaiety that amazed her, she put on a smiling face even when she saw Christy clinging to Brand's side. Although he continued with his chores and didn't encourage the woman, he also didn't fight her attentions.

When the entertainment ended and the crowd began to disperse, Brand joined Dayna. His hand gently touched her shoulder, and his caressing blue eyes stared down at her. Without a word, Shelly and Martin squeezed closer together to give Brand room to lift his leg over the bench and slide in next to her.

The faint scent of his after-shave lotion titillated Dayna's senses as his shoulder rubbed hers intimately and his thigh pressed against hers beneath the bench table. She was conscious of an overpowering force rising up in her while he chatted casually about the western dinner. But all the time his eyes were sending hers outrageously bold messages and his lips were smiling with unspoken words that had nothing to do with his conversation. "Did you enjoy tonight?"

"Yes. It was fun. You have hidden talents."

A low, amused chuckle answered her. "So have you," he said, with a devilish grin. "How about a moonlight walk?" He didn't wait for a reply. As soon as she was standing beside him, he slid an arm around her shoulders, nestling her close to the curve of his side. She wrapped her arm around the broad expanse of his back as they ambled over the flagstone walkway and down toward the pool.

Gesturing at some small palm trees that formed an enormous umbrella for the chairs beneath their fronds, Brand drew her even closer. "Let's go down to the trees."

When they reached their destination, he leaned against one of the palms and pulled her into the security of his arms. His hands pressed against her back, so that her body leaned suggestively against him. Dayna ached to stay close to him, hold him, and never have to say goodbye. She felt the hard, thudding beat of his heart against her breast as he gripped her fiercely to him. The warmth of his breath stirred against her temple, and his fingers gently stroked the small of her back as she looked up at the dark sky. "It's so beautiful."

Brand answered distractedly, taking a deep breath and inhaling the fragrance of her light perfume, "Uh huh." His bland comment caught her attention and she drew back. "You're not even looking up."

"I'm looking at what I'm interested in." Teasingly, he nibbled her ear. His voice was soft and provocative. "Would you like to see my etchings?"

A delighted smile curved Dayna's lips at such a hackneyed line. "Etchings of what?"

He pondered for a second, a smile deepening the lines at the corners of his eyes. "Which would you believe—etchings of horses or skyscrapers?"

Dayna rolled her eyes upward in mock disbelief. "Neither."

He clicked his tongue and shook his head. "I'm wounded to the quick."

"Well, are they pastels or oils?" she asked coyly.

His eyes sparkled with amused pleasure. "Interested in culture," he asked, glancing at his watch, "at twelve-thirty in the morning?"

Dayna brushed her lips across his cheek. "Any time is a good time to be educated," she said softly in his ear.

Later, in Brand's room, they found a new dimension to their lovemaking, a fierceness and a hunger, as if they both sensed that the joy they'd known for the last few days would slowly slip from their grasp.

Still wrapped in the rapture they had just shared, Dayna was filled with an unexplainable joy, a contented peace of mind. Unnoticed, tears slipped from the corners of her eyes. Brand lifted himself slightly from her as their moistness touched his cheek. "Did I hurt you?"

Dayna shook her head, unable to say anything.

"Are they sad tears?" he asked in a husky whisper. She shook her head again and he held her even more tightly to him. "I'm glad you decided to throw your sensible caution to the winds."

She caressed the nape of his neck and his bare back. "I know—destiny," she finally said. "What makes you think I have?"

Lying beside her, he frowned in puzzlement. "Haven't you?"

"No, I've just learned to accept things more realistically."

"You're serious, aren't you?" he asked, sitting up slightly and shoving a pillow behind his back. "What do you mean by realistically?" he asked as Dayna slipped from the bed and began to dress.

She shrugged, hoping she wouldn't weaken and succumb to the notions of love that were an inseparable part of her ideas about sex. "I told you, I don't romanticize relationships. What we've shared has been very wonderful, but it's also the result of a very primitive drive."

"Why do you think that's all it is?"

"Because it happened too fast. Your persistence won out, that's all."

"I'm not solely responsible for what's happened. You're here because of your feelings. You've been falling in love with me since the moment we met. That's what you're afraid of facing, and you don't want to admit it."

"No, I'm not. I know what I feel," she answered firmly, turning toward him as she sat on the edge of the bed.

"Are you afraid of love?"

"No, but I know it doesn't happen this quickly. It doesn't just hit people. What we're sharing has no lasting quality. There hasn't been enough time."

His gaze clashed with hers. Dayna squared her shoulders, sure she was in control of her life and the outcome of their relationship. His features suddenly became gentle and his gaze much softer; Dayna felt some of her control slipping. Weakened just by his look, she sensed the need to make her point now, before he reached out and touched her. "It's easy to confuse purely physical attraction for love. But love is built on common interests and on truly knowing a person. Love can't happen in a matter of hours or days. It takes time."

"It can happen in minutes," Brand said with complete certainty, as he reached out for her arm. He drew her, fully dressed by now, back down to the bed.

He stared down at her, the weight of his body holding her firmly beneath him. Dayna knew she wasn't going to be able to leave yet. His mouth tantalized the side of her neck. "You are a very wise lady," he mumbled as his lips settled on the curve of her shoulder, "but you're wrong this time. You are in love with me."

She closed her eyes, her hands sliding over his back. Doubts of her own wisdom began to stir. He never backed down. Was it possible he was right? Was the emotion they shared really love?

His hand slipped beneath her skirt and gently stroked her leg with teasing slowness, sending renewed sensations through her as his strong fingers moved over her inner thigh. She tried to resist the emotions he was intent on arousing again and halfheartedly insisted, "Brand, I should leave."

"You don't want to." He held her beneath him, his moist tongue sliding over her collarbone.

The knock on the door was like being doused with a bucket of cold water. Dayna's skirt was hitched high on her thigh, and she was afraid that someone might enter without permission and find them in compromising intimacy.

She scampered off the bed, pulling up the strap of her dress and smoothing down the skirt as Brand quickly slipped from the bed and grabbed a robe from the closet. Wild sensations were still coursing through her as she watched while he slid the robe over his bare body. Tying it, he moved toward the door.

"I would have come sooner but . . ." Christy's sultry voice stopped as she caught sight of Dayna. "I'm sorry. Did I interrupt something?"

Christy's remark reverberated through the room, every word giving her a painful jolt. Dayna didn't look at Brand. Remembering Brand's brief conversation with Christy after the rodeo, Dayna was convinced he had made an arrangement with her instead.

Self-disgust sent her flying past him, and though Brand's hand flashed out to stop her, like a female tigress she emitted a threatening growl, her green eyes smoldering with the pain and anger of humiliation.

"Dayna, stop! Wait a minute."

She brushed past Christy in the doorway, nearly knocking her over. Dayna didn't care. She stumbled in her haste as she ran up the hill toward the lodge. Using the pool area as a shortcut, she caught herself on some of the bushes, scratching her arm. She winced, but the pain was insignificant in comparison with the agonizing ache suffusing her whole body. Pressing her hand across her mouth to muffle sobs, she paused. The sound of men's voices speaking in hushed whispers made her linger in the bushes.

She recognized one of the voices as Cutler's as he whispered, "Hurry up. We've only got ten minutes to meet them."

Dayna sniffed back a sob, waiting until she heard a truck engine and the sound of the tires squealing before she came out of the shrubbery. Wryly, she wondered what party they were heading for. Or maybe, she thought with an ironic frown, Cutler forgot the beer for the poker game. Either way, it seemed to be a night of fun and games for every-one. Only some of the games weren't so funny.

Chapter Ten

*M*ercifully, Karen and Shelly were asleep when Dayna reached the room. She struggled against her pride and found herself shaking, every nerve in her body jumping. Closeting herself in the bathroom, she moved to the sink to wash her face. A madwoman stared back at her from the sink mirror. Her face was smudged, her hair in wild disarray, her clothes disheveled. She nearly burst into hysterical laughter at her reflection—she must have been insane to weaken and almost believe his claim of love. Fool! she mentally screamed.

It seemed that hours passed before she calmed down. She showered and then slid into a thin batiste nightgown and brushed her hair. It was well past three in the morning before she fell asleep, only to reawaken during the remaining dark hours.

Giving up all hope of any further sleep when she saw by her travel clock that it was five-thirty, she got up. Dawn was breaking as she quietly dressed.

She left the room and walked softly through the long hall to the stairway. The lobby was empty and quiet. As she descended the stairs, she heard early-morning noises coming from the kitchen and headed in that direction.

Charlie and two helpers were busy with preparations for breakfast; Charlie himself was rapidly beating a giant bowl of batter. He greeted her with a bright smile and offered to make her breakfast right then if she wanted it. Dayna refused the heavy waffles and ham he suggested. She knew they would have stuck in her throat. Last night had been a disaster, and she was still feeling its aftereffects, a heavy heart and a splitting headache.

Charlie's voice penetrated her thoughts. "Missy Dayna?"

Dayna's head snapped in his direction.

"Coffee, Charlie. Would that be all right?"

With hurried, short steps, he moved to the stove to get her a cup.

Dayna sat in the kitchen for only a few minutes, exchanging pleasantries with Charlie while he worked. Then, pulling on her corduroy blazer, she walked slowly down to the stables. It was a beautiful time of day, with half the sky still gray as streaks of orange light started to break the horizon.

Her decision to ride was the result of a need to feel the wind blowing through her hair, to feel some kind of freedom from the oppressive pain inside her.

As she neared the stables, Bonnie appeared. Surprised to find him there so early, Dayna queried, "Don't you ever sleep?"

"Could ask you the same," he said with a grin. "You're up mighty early. But then so are a lot of people around here. Brand's been in town since three this morning."

Dayna couldn't stop herself—her curiosity got the better of her. "Why?"

"We had quite a ruckus here a couple of hours ago. Do you remember that fellow Brand fired about two weeks ago?" Dayna didn't know him, but she remembered hearing some mention of a man Brand had had trouble with. "Caught him and John Cutler in the act of rustling about four this morning. Brand's been down at the sheriff's office ever since. They caught some buddies of theirs in another truck just this side of Douglas, driving a truckload of stolen cattle."

Her thin brow arched in response to his words. So she had been right in her suspicions about Cutler. If Brand had listened to her he might have saved himself a lot of aggravation. She looked away in self-disgust, wishing she didn't care so much about him.

Bonnie tipped his head to the side, eyeing her questioningly. She knew he was puzzled over her silence, but she couldn't concentrate on anything except that she had been right about Brand Renfrow and the type of man he was right from the beginning. Last night had proved that. She wondered wryly if she had witnessed Cutler and his partner in crime in the act of leaving to commit their criminal act. There was no way of knowing for certain if she had.

"You know, Brand never liked Cutler," Bonnie commented offhandedly. "But he gave him a fair chance. His judgment about people is usually pretty sound. And if you ask any of the ranch hands, they'll tell you he's fair and real straight with them." Dayna said nothing, thinking it was too bad Brand wasn't as honest with women. "Well," Bonnie said with exaggerated lightness, "so how come you're up so early?"

Dayna gave a shrug. "I couldn't sleep."

He grinned wryly. "Watch out. You might get into the habit of these early mornings. That's what happened to me. Got used to breaking camp by four in the morning on cattle drives. Can't sleep later now."

Trying to gain greater control of the emotional turmoil inside her and hide the sadness she felt, she said with feigned lightheartedness, "I'm sure I'll slide right back into my lazy morning routine once I return home." Before Bonnie could make any further comment, she asked, "Could I have the bay, please? I want to go for a ride."

Saying nothing more, Bonnie turned away to saddle and bridle the bay.

Bringing the horse out to her, he sent a worried frown in her direction. "You be careful. It's awfully early to be out riding."

"I will," Dayna answered, taking the reins from him.

"I'm surprised such a little lady as yourself took to such a big horse," Bonnie commented.

"He's gentle." She patted the horse.

"Oh, that he is, but women don't usually like them this big."

"Brand picked him out." Dayna remembered the day he had come from the stables leading the horse he'd chosen for her.

"You look mighty sad, Dayna."

Dayna smiled slightly. "Do you know that's the first time, Bonnie, you've called me by my name."

"Well, you're such a slender, wispy-looking thing, I guess I kind of tagged you with 'little lady,' but that doesn't mean I don't know your name," he said in a voice that made Dayna look at him. "Especially with Brand saying it daily."

Dayna's heart skipped at his words. "He mentioned me to you?"

"Little lady, I told you once before you bothered him. Oh, he never has said outright what he feels. But he'd ask me where you were or what you were doing. And I've never known him to care like that about any lady before."

Her brows knitted with confusion. Bonnie's expression was enigmatic. Dayna's eyes shifted to the mountains in the distance. Pointing an arm toward them she asked, "Would it be all right if I ride that way?"

Bonnie made a face. "I don't think you should. It's not good to just ride off somewhere unless you know the land real well. There's a lot of it out there. Why don't you ride one of the trails? That way you won't have any trouble coming back."

"No," Dayna countered, feeling rebellious. "I don't want to. I've been that way. I want to see something different," she said, her annoyance with

Bonnie's solicitous attitude very apparent in her sharp tone.

Showing his distress, Bonnie appealed, "Dayna, I don't think you should."

Adamantly, she declared, "Well, I will." With a quick pull she turned the horse away from Bonnie and sent it into a gallop.

Behind her, Bonnie muttered, "Dagnabit—stubborn female!"

How long Dayna rode, she didn't know. She slowed the horse once the ranch disappeared from view. As the bay dawdled along she tried to straighten out her feelings. She had been a fool where Brand was concerned. Christy's appearance forced her to face how little she really meant to him.

She raised her eyes to see where she was. Without a guiding hand, the horse had headed for the greenest place he knew—the same stand of palm trees where she and Brand had nearly made love. She slid off the saddle and walked the horse to one of the palms. After tying him to the tree, she wandered absently about, picking some of the pastel-hued wildflowers. With the flowers in her lap, she sat cross-legged under the tree. Memories of the kisses, the feel of Brand's arms around her, the thrilling shiver he could send through her body with his touch floated back to her. How could he have become so much a part of her in two short weeks? It was as if she had known him all her life, as if there could be no life without him.

The thought brought her swiftly to her feet. She squeezed her eyes shut, as if by doing so she could block out such thoughts. For the sake of your pride, she argued to herself, you can't love him. But her thoughts were overshadowed by the sound of horse's hooves in the distance. Turning toward it, she saw a rider on a chestnut quarter horse approaching.

Her body tensed, her mind warning her, as Brand drew closer. For all the angry determination coursing through her, she felt her legs go weak beneath her just at the sight of him. She knew she was outmatched by the commanding, imposing man who was now almost at her side. What Brand couldn't convey with words, he could prove in a much more physical manner, one that she had no defenses against.

Her anger became heavily intermingled with sensual excitement as she watched him slide from the saddle and stride toward her. "What are you doing, going off like that?" he snapped angrily.

"Bonnie's got a big mouth," she remarked just as testily.

"He did right. If he hadn't told me, he would have been in big trouble." His angry blue eyes stared down at her. "What if you got lost? Then what?"

Her voice crackled with proud emotion. "I know where I am! Look around," she flared, "or don't you remember?"

Brand gave the area only a fleeting glance but his features softened, indicating that he remembered the day they'd spent there. His eyes returned to her and the gentleness she saw warned her to run from him.

As he drew near, Dayna avoided the disarming

quality of his gaze by staring down at the wildflowers in her hand. As he reached out to caress her chin, she pulled back slightly as if recoiling from his touch.

"I didn't invite her," Brand growled.

She had expected the very words she had just heard and avoided responding to them. "I understand you were at the sheriff's office this morning." She dared to look up at him. His mouth was set in a thin, hard, determined line; he was aware she was diverting the conversation to a less personal topic. "Seems I was right about Cutler," she couldn't help adding.

"Yes, you were," Brand admitted. He took a step closer and Dayna tensed. His blue eyes had narrowed, glints of confidence and impatience flashing in them. "We'd already suspected Cutler though."

Dayna murmured with some surprise, "You did?"

"We've been waiting for the past five days for him to make a move, but I didn't want you involved in any way. That's why I played it down when you told W.R. and me yesterday morning about what you'd overheard."

"You really knew?"

Brand nodded. "Cutler had Mexican connections and was smuggling the cattle across the state line. He was pretty sly. He'd stay at a ranch for a while, gain his employer's trust, and then make his move." His voice suddenly went soft, his mind as one-tracked as ever. "Dayna, I didn't invite her. She came on her own. The only woman I want in

my arms is you." His breath warmed her face,
suffocating her with his nearness, and the thoughts
about Christy that had seemed so important just
seconds ago slipped away, forgotten in the wave of
weakness that flooded her. His voice caressed her.
"I want you." He leaned even closer and bent his
head. As his lips gently followed the dainty contour
of her ear, Dayna closed her eyes, giving in to the
whirling sensation that swept through her. The
wildflowers fell from her hand to the ground as the
steel band of his arm encircled her waist and pulled
her body against the length of his. His lips brushed
hers and then pressed down, moving with slow
deliberation and thorough passion. When he drew
his head back, his voice was thick with emotion.
"You know I want you. Only you. Now, show me
you love me before it's too late."

He wanted her, only her. A sense of what he was
really saying seeped through the intoxicating spell
that bound her. But then her mind completed the
thought. He wanted her only for now. Not forever.
She tensed beneath the smoldering touch of his lips
on her neck and denied the desire that was consuming her, knowing she couldn't allow herself to
succumb again. She pushed him away. Brand said
nothing, but from the corner of her eye Dayna saw
his dark frown. She jumped beneath the touch of
his hand on her cheek as he gently swept her hair
back to view her face better. Afraid she would
unwittingly blurt out the words that could completely weaken her, she spun away and ran to her
horse, quickly mounting before Brand could reach
her. He made a wild grab for the bridle, but she
nipped the horse's flanks, and holding on firmly to

keep from being unseated, she urged the horse to a wild gallop and headed back to the ranch.

With the sound of thundering hooves behind her, fear rose within her. She hadn't expected Brand's pursuit, and she wanted nothing more than to avoid another encounter with him. She brought the horse to a sliding stop, much to the dismay of Bonnie, who stood nearby inside the corral. Dayna didn't give the ranch hands in the corral more than a flickering glance.

Dismounting quickly, she glanced back and saw that Brand was nearly there. Hurrying the horse toward one of the men, she handed him the reins. "Here," she demanded, "take care of him."

She turned away but froze as Brand slid his quarter horse to a halt frighteningly close to her, jumped from the horse, and grabbed her arm before she could escape.

The men were startled at the sight of their foreman's hell-bent actions. Brand didn't notice the audience. His face was hard with determination, and Dayna desperately tried to break free.

His fingers tightened on her arm in a viselike grip as she tried to pull away. From the corner of her eye, she saw Bonnie storming toward the men and heard his harsh reprimand. "You fellows got nothing to do but stand around here? I'll find you some work. That's what W.R. pays you for, not to put your nose in other people's business."

As Bonnie hustled them out of hearing range, Brand grabbed both her arms and whirled her around to face him. With a courage she didn't feel, Dayna met the anger in his narrowed blue eyes. The impatience consuming him was even more evident in his voice. "Did you think if you ran off that would be the end of it?"

A combination of fear and anxiety left her breathless and her voice weak. "There's nothing more to say. Christy's appearance last night and your actions now say more than enough."

"You're wrong! Maybe you think everything is nice and clear, but I don't. There's a lot more to be said." He drew a deep breath, trying to calm himself. "Christy is *Cutler's* girlfriend. Her job was to pander to my ego and especially to make sure I was kept busy last night." Dayna saw a muscle in his jaw twitch, conveying how angry he was although he kept his voice low. "You just couldn't trust me, could you? And I understand why, now."

"Trust—like everything else—needs time to grow," Dayna responded.

"Time!" he scoffed. "What you really mean is you've never believed anything I've ever said. You've assumed everything I've said has been some—some ploy to get you to bed."

"You just asked me again to make love with you before it was too late," she said softly.

Brand hissed, not wanting to be heard. "I got that kind of love from you days ago," he reminded her bluntly. "I didn't mean just physical love. But you know that. You've wrapped me up in knots, but you don't care because that's what you intended to do."

Dayna looked up now. His eyes pierced her like sharp knives. The weight of his anger bore down on her as he released his hold on her so abruptly she stumbled back a step. "Hank overheard your little plan to teach me a lesson. But I never wanted to believe that's what you were doing. *You* aren't a damn fool. *I* am!''

Dayna found her voice, but her words suddenly sounded weak even to her own ears. "I didn't want to be used. I told you before, whirlwind romances don't last."

He released a bitter laugh. "You've done a fine job of proving you were right. You haven't been used. But I have. Because, like a fool, I fell in love with you, when all the time none of it meant anything to you."

His words came at her like a powerful bolt of lightning. Dayna laid a trembling hand to her mouth to prevent her emotions from breaking loose. Through blurred vision, she watched Brand whirl away, his irate strides carrying him quickly toward the big house. As he disappeared from her sight, the door closing behind him, she was still dazed, still too stunned to utter a defense. Christy had been part of the rustling scheme. Had Brand known that, too? Had he deliberately allowed her to make a play for him so that Cutler wouldn't become suspicious? But one thing was certain. She had used him. By denying her love for him and the love he professed for her, she had been emotionally destructive to him. Slowly, she became aware of her surroundings and the curious stares of the ranch hands, who had overheard some of Brand's outburst. She squared her shoulders and stumbled inside trying to salvage some dignity despite the shattering effects of the scene that had just ended. She stood trembling in her room, knowing that as much as she loved him, she had unwittingly hurt him.

Dayna burrowed herself under the sheet, not wanting to get out of bed, not wanting to face the morning and what it eventually would bring. She placed the pillow over her head but still heard Shelly's muffled voice. Knowing she couldn't escape the inevitable by such childish actions, she rolled onto her back with a soft moan, jarred to wakefulness by the sight of Karen packing. It was a sharp reminder that they were leaving in a few hours. Seats had been reserved for them on a late afternoon flight, so she had only the morning and early afternoon left. Somehow she'd arrived at a decision while she slept.

Brand had been absent all day yesterday, and pride had kept Dayna from asking anyone where he was. Pride, it seemed, had caused her more harm than good, for it was just that need to maintain her self-respect at all costs that had prevented her from believing his words of love. A restless night had dispelled every emotion but one—love. She loved him. That was all that was important now.

Both Shelly's and Karen's eyes were on her as she sat up and commented wryly, "I think I could have slept all day."

Returning her attention to the suitcase she was packing, Karen quipped, "That would be a good way to miss the flight."

Dayna appealed, "Karen, don't. The last thing I need is unasked-for advice."

"Sure," Karen mumbled.

Trying to lighten the mood, Dayna looked at Shelly, who appeared to be uncomfortable because of the irritated sound of her friends' exchange. "Well, Shelly, some cowpoke didn't sweep you into his arms and ride off into the sunset with you, but an accountant did. Did Martin talk of continuing this romance?"

Shelly shook off her discomfort and beamed. "He did say Chicago and New York aren't so far apart." Shyly, she admitted, "He also said he was seriously considering relocating to Chicago."

Karen whirled around in response to the unexpected news, and she smiled with happiness for her friend. "Oh, Shelly, that's great!"

As if she was trying to keep the joy she felt subdued, Shelly nodded and said quietly, "Yes, it really is."

Dayna rose from the bed and stepped forward to give Shelly a hug. "I'm happy for you."

Keeping her eyes intent on the blouse she was folding, Karen remarked, "Arizona, however, isn't just a jump away from Chicago. I doubt if we'll ever see anyone from here again." Getting no reaction from Dayna, Karen added, "Dayna, what are you doing? Are you really going to be able to forget Brand the minute you step on board the plane today?" Dayna made a move as if to stop her, but Karen seemed determined to say what was on her mind. "He's in love with you. Tell him you love him. You haven't, have you?"

"I'm going to," Dayna answered quietly.

"What?"

She smiled at Karen's dumbfounded expression

and explained as she gestured toward her suitcase, "I'm only packing in case I'm forced to leave. I've hurt him. He may have decided I'm not worth all the trouble."

For the next two hours, Dayna searched everywhere for Brand. She didn't care who knew of her desperate need to find Brand, but by noon, her hope was fading. Brand was nowhere to be found. Heading back to the lodge, she glanced at her wristwatch. Only two hours were left before her flight. Despondently, she entered the lobby, knowing she had to pack. She'd do a hurried job and use any time left to continue what appeared to be a futile search.

She began to climb the stairs when the door of W.R.'s office opened. Leaning against the door-frame, he called out to her, "Dayna, may I speak with you?"

She nodded, but her heart lurched with apprehension when she saw the grim expression on his face as she entered his office.

W.R. closed the door behind her. "Please sit here," he said, indicating the chair Dayna had seen Brand slouching lazily in many times throughout the past two weeks.

She sat down and ran her hands over the leather of the chair, wondering if this was as close to Brand as she would ever get again.

Bluntly he stated, "You're looking for Brand."

Dayna nodded. "I've looked everywhere. No one seems to know where he is." With a cheerless laugh, she said, "He's doing another disappearing act I guess."

"No, he isn't, Dayna. I know where he is. He

told me last night he was riding out and wouldn't be back until late this afternoon."

"Is it far?" Thinking of making a desperate attempt to see him, she said, "Maybe I'd have time to ride out there."

He shook his head. "No, it's too far. Dayna, it was deliberate. He didn't want to be around today."

Her throat constricted as tears began to form.

"I'm sorry," W.R. said with a frown. "He just didn't want to be here when you left."

"I wanted to tell him that . . ." The words caught in her throat.

Lines were etched deeply in W.R.'s face, and Dayna tried to gain hold of her composure.

"Dayna, Brand was in such a state yesterday I told him that if he didn't tell me what was going on I'd hogtie him to a chair," he said, revealing the concern he was feeling over the situation.

"Did—did he tell you?"

"No, he refused. But anyone watching you two could see the love that was growing between you. I just wish he'd regain his good sense and get back here before it's too late."

Drawing a deep, ragged breath, Dayna glanced at the clock on the wall behind W.R.'s chair. W.R.'s words echoed in her mind as the clock ticked away precious minutes. Everyone had seen their love but her. "I think it might already be too late."

The bustling airport sounds were nerve-racking to Dayna as she awaited the dreaded announcement to board their flight. With a heavy sigh,

Bonnie set their luggage on the floor. "Sure don't want to say goodbye." Somewhat self-consciously, he moved the rim of his hat between his fingers. "It's like you belonged at the ranch. Kind of thought you might be there all the time, Dayna. W.R. would be real happy if you came back. Me, too."

Dayna raised a bemused face to him as she tried to sort out all her confused thoughts. Suddenly, she reached a decision. She turned to Karen. "You can handle anything that comes up at the travel agency, can't you?"

"Yes," Karen answered quickly. "You're going back?"

Dayna nodded. "I'm going back. Brand isn't the only one who never gives up. This is too important for me to just walk away. I have to talk to him again."

Bonnie's face brightened agreeably but a familiar voice behind her interrupted. "Now that sounds like my strong-willed daughter."

Dayna whirled around in surprise, not believing her ears.

"Dad, what are you doing here?"

"I came to visit an old friend," Edward Palmer offered with a smile.

Dayna's face had a dubious expression. "You just left the business to come here? Needed to see W.R. that badly, did you?"

"I just closed the office for the day," he said placatingly. "Karen will be there to handle matters tomorrow." Dayna's green eyes leveled a curious look at him, forcing him to answer more truthfully. "When I talked to you on the phone, you sounded as if for the first time since you were twenty, you might need me."

Dayna smiled, placing an affectionate hand on his arm. "For a while it seemed I'd lost direction. Now I know exactly what I'm going to do."

Neither he nor Dayna said a word all the way back to the ranch. Her stomach was churning with apprehension, afraid that despite her hopes, Brand would turn a cold, hard gaze on her again and walk away. Bonnie, however, was unbelievably light-spirited, grinning the whole time and offering them a whistled repertoire of country and western songs.

As the van made the final turn into the dusty road and the ranch came into view, Bonnie abruptly brought the vehicle to a stop.

The white stallion came thundering across the desert at a gallop, hooves flying and stirring up puffs of dirt. The rider altered his direction, approaching the van. Edward Palmer cast a worried frown at the man riding toward them but urged, "Talk to him, Dayna."

Her stomach flipped over as she opened the van door. Hesitantly, she moved toward the dust cloud, but the rumbling sound of an engine caused her to turn around. She watched Bonnie driving away, leaving her stranded and waiting for her only means of transportation to the ranch.

Brand reined the stallion to a halt only inches away from her. From his lofty position on the huge horse, he demanded, "What are you doing here? I thought you'd left."

Struggling to maintain a calm exterior, she said with false brightness, "I missed my plane."

His brow furrowed. "How? Bonnie has never

missed getting people off on time. How the . . . ?"
Understanding lit up his blue eyes, but they continued to scrutinize her warily. Her courage was ready
to fly from her and her heart hammered thunder-
ously in her chest, but she stood with a firm, rigid
posture, facing his skeptical regard.

He appeared very relaxed, leaning forward to
pat the mane of the horse, who was showing
impatience at having to stand still. "But Shelly and
Karen made it on time?"

"Uh huh," she answered weakly.

A long, considering look held her paralyzed
before he said, "Come here."

Dayna obeyed his command. In one swift movement he leaned over, slipped an arm securely
around her waist, and lifted her to the space in
front of him on the saddle. Dayna held her breath
and looked down at the sun-browned arms
wrapped around her waist and the hand lightly
holding the reins. Love rushed through her as she
remembered all the times she'd known his gentle
tenderness, not just while making love but every
time he touched her reassuringly or protectively.
The warmth of his body so close to hers and his
male scent were stimulating. She yearned to lean
back and lay her head on his shoulder and feel the
heat of his breath on her face.

When they reached the lodge, he dismounted
and helped her down. His penetrating blue eyes
bore into her. "Why did you come back?"

Dayna flinched inwardly at the hardness in his
voice. "Please," she appealed softly, "we have to
talk."

The warmth of his hands left her waist and with them went some of her courage.

A cold chill swept over her at his next words. "I thought we already had." His eyes clouded with confusion. "Why? Why did you think I considered every woman I met easy prey?" Bemusement deepened his frown, knitting his fair brows. "I don't have any list of conquests."

"You came on to me right from the start. What *could* I think?" she managed to answer, hoping he wasn't as proud as she had been and would be able to understand.

"My mistake was thinking you were the most beautiful, most desirable woman I'd ever met. Maybe I did come on too strong when we first met. That's my problem, not yours," he said, showing his irritation with himself.

Dayna tried to make him understand. "I overheard what you said to W.R. You were so arrogant, so sure you could handle me like every other woman."

"Are you talking about when you first arrived?" At Dayna's affirmative nod, he added, "That's what made you think I chased every skirt that arrived at the ranch?"

Dayna couldn't meet the piercing blue eyes staring down at her. "That and—well, you have to remember I didn't know then that you weren't the man Alexandria Minter complained about. And," she hesitated, finding it difficult to be as open as he was, "it was obvious you were skilled at getting your own way."

He heaved a deep sigh. "I said that to W.R. for your benefit. I knew you were eavesdropping."

Dayna closed her eyes for a moment, trying to clear her mind of the confusion muddling it. "But W.R. said . . ."

Brand interjected, "He knows how much I like a woman with spirit. That's all he meant. He probably could see the obstinacy in you and was just offering advice."

She hesitated and then looked up. "And you knew all along that Christy was just . . ."

"Trying to make a fool of me?" he finished. "Yes, I knew."

Dayna took a deep breath, his smile giving her the encouragement she needed. "W.R. said you wouldn't be back until evening."

"I don't know how to give up," he answered with a trace of self-derision. "I thought maybe you hadn't left yet."

"I don't know how to give up, either. But it's happening so fast, Brand. It's frightening. I'm afraid," she admitted honestly.

A wariness crept into his gaze. "Of course you are." His voice was filled with understanding. "Isn't everyone, a little bit?"

"You aren't," Dayna said lightly, forcing a weak smile.

"Sure I am." He was silent for a minute, and Dayna wanted to erase the frown from his face. "There isn't any woman, Dayna; I'd admit that to no one but the one I loved and trusted. I told you right from the start it was love at first sight."

"I thought it was a line," she admitted ruefully. "How could you be so sure?"

"I'm not a kid. I know the difference. You should have, too. Why would you be concerned about a man getting into trouble with his employer, or worry about him getting hurt, or hate the sight of him with another woman, if all you're interested in is his body?"

Dayna nodded her head and sighed. "I guess that's true. You know I kissed you and made love with you because of a much deeper interest. And what Hank heard me say, I said in a moment of anger to Karen. But I never played games with you. I never did. You have to believe that. I was confused. So many times I wanted to believe it was real, but it seemed like a whirlwind romance we had both rushed into."

"I told you I loved you," he insisted.

"Oh, Brand, you don't know how much I wanted to believe you really did. And at the rodeo when I watched you, I knew I was in love with you, but I still found it hard to believe that what you said was true. I started to believe it, then, but Christy came in and . . ."

An eternity of silence followed while his eyes searched her face. "Say it again," he demanded.

"I love you."

He swept her into the warmth of his embrace. "One more time," he requested, his arms tightening around her back. Dayna heard the warmth in his voice and tilted her head back. His lips played over hers, brushing across them, kissing their edges as she mouthed the words he wanted to hear.

"This ranch," he mumbled, "needs a woman's touch."

"Oh," Dayna commented wryly, glancing around her. "I think it's done very well so far."

"Don't argue," he said with soft laughter.

"I can't promise never to argue with you again."

"Lord, I hope not," Brand replied as Dayna brushed her cheek against his jaw. "It's that stubbornness in those green eyes that first caught my attention that day at the hotel in Phoenix. That and the way you met my stare head on and gave me the same kind of once-over I gave you."

"You were looking for an easy pickup," Dayna chided teasingly.

His breath tickled the inner contour of her ear. "If you use the word 'casual,' I'll . . ."

"You'll what?" Dayna mockingly challenged and drew back to see his eyes. Suffused with a radiant glow she gave him no chance to answer. She stood on her toes and initiated another kiss, this time one that grew urgent not only with passion but with the love they had shared and previously denied. They were breathless as the sound of hooves clumping over the sand broke the spell.

Drawing a deep breath, Brand smiled tenderly down at her. The sight of his loving gaze spread a wave of warm and thrilling excitement through her. She watched him reluctantly tear his gaze from her as a ranch hand cleared his throat and stared at the ground in embarrassment.

Brand greeted him with an indulgent smile. "It better be important, Hank."

Hank smiled wryly. "I'm sorry to bother you, Boss. But they just delivered the gelding you were expecting, and I tried to sign for him, but they won't take my signature. They insist on the owner's signature. I've looked all over for W.R.," he said with an apologetic shrug, "but I can't find your uncle anywhere. Will you sign these?" he asked, thrusting some papers at Brand.

Dayna pulled away. No words passed between them, but as Brand moved forward and took the papers and pen, Dayna saw his deeply etched frown.

Slowly she followed, chiding herself for being so slow to recognize that the Double R stood for Reardon and Renfrow. She moved close to Brand and looked over his arm at the papers. His blue eyes glanced up at her sheepishly before he concentrated on the papers and swiftly scrawled his strong masculine signature on the appropriate line.

Handing the papers to the ranch hand, Brand asked, "You checked him over good, didn't you?"

"Sure did, Boss."

"Okay, I'll be down in a little while to see him."

Brand turned to Dayna as Hank rode away with the signed papers. She no longer needed an explanation. "The white stallion is yours," she said. "Half of this ranch is yours," she added with an exaggerated sweep of her arm, "isn't it, *Boss?*"

He chuckled softly and reached out, pulling her close again. "It would just have complicated things more than they already were if I had told you." Dayna leaned against his hard body, unable to remain indignant when she heard the pain in his voice as he added softly, "It hurts to love someone and not have that love returned."

"I know," she agreed, placing her hands on his

neck, one hand caressing the strong line of his jaw.

Brand silenced any further remarks and drew her into his embrace. "From here on, we join forces. Forever," he mumbled, his mouth descending on hers, possessing her with a kiss.

MORE ROMANCE FOR
A SPECIAL WAY TO RELAX
$1.95 each

2 ☐ Hastings	23 ☐ Charles	45 ☐ Charles	66 ☐ Mikels
3 ☐ Dixon	24 ☐ Dixon	46 ☐ Howard	67 ☐ Shaw
4 ☐ Vitek	25 ☐ Hardy	47 ☐ Stephens	68 ☐ Sinclair
5 ☐ Converse	26 ☐ Scott	48 ☐ Ferrell	69 ☐ Dalton
6 ☐ Douglass	27 ☐ Wisdom	49 ☐ Hastings	70 ☐ Clare
7 ☐ Stanford	28 ☐ Ripy	50 ☐ Browning	71 ☐ Skillern
8 ☐ Halston	29 ☐ Bergen	51 ☐ Trent	72 ☐ Belmont
9 ☐ Baxter	30 ☐ Stephens	52 ☐ Sinclair	73 ☐ Taylor
10 ☐ Thiels	31 ☐ Baxter	53 ☐ Thomas	74 ☐ Wisdom
11 ☐ Thornton	32 ☐ Douglass	54 ☐ Hohl	75 ☐ John
12 ☐ Sinclair	33 ☐ Palmer	55 ☐ Stanford	76 ☐ Ripy
13 ☐ Beckman	35 ☐ James	56 ☐ Wallace	77 ☐ Bergen
14 ☐ Keene	36 ☐ Dailey	57 ☐ Thornton	78 ☐ Gladstone
15 ☐ James	37 ☐ Stanford	58 ☐ Douglass	79 ☐ Hastings
16 ☐ Carr	38 ☐ John	59 ☐ Roberts	80 ☐ Douglass
17 ☐ John	39 ☐ Milan	60 ☐ Thorne	81 ☐ Thornton
18 ☐ Hamilton	40 ☐ Converse	61 ☐ Beckman	82 ☐ McKenna
19 ☐ Shaw	41 ☐ Halston	62 ☐ Bright	83 ☐ Major
20 ☐ Musgrave	42 ☐ Drummond	63 ☐ Wallace	84 ☐ Stephens
21 ☐ Hastings	43 ☐ Shaw	64 ☐ Converse	85 ☐ Beckman
22 ☐ Howard	44 ☐ Eden	65 ☐ Cates	86 ☐ Halston

If you enjoyed this book...

...you will enjoy a Special Edition Book Club membership even more.

It will bring you each new title, as soon as it is published every month, delivered right to your door.

15-Day Free Trial Offer

We will send you 6 new Silhouette Special Editions to keep for 15 days absolutely free! If you decide not to keep them, send them back to us, you pay nothing. But if you enjoy them as much as we think you will, keep them and pay the invoice enclosed with your trial shipment. You will then automatically become a member of the Special Edition Book Club and receive 6 more romances every month. There is no minimum number of books to buy and you can cancel at any time.

READERS' COMMENTS ON SILHOUETTE SPECIAL EDITIONS: